*To Peter. Things left unsaid ended
something that never had a
chance to really begin.*

Prologue

Iona

The restrictions held so tightly by the SLAG Nation has been compromised. More and more demons invade the Real stealing the near lifeless body of unsuspecting coma patients. The Dark Lord struck a deal the SLAGs truly believed had been for the greater good. Though they regretted the accord, they were powerless to break it without cause. The Dark Lord worked such an accord that left much open to interpretation. This was what he used to his advantage. The only hope was that the Kingdom Council find a way to revoke the accord and bring balance yet again back to both worlds.

The Accord as documented by the SLAG Nation:

Lord Soubackalou of the Shadowland has petitioned the SLAG Nation for entry into the Realm with express concern about the overwhelming unbalance of power being observed by the continued travel between the Realm and the Real of Nadine, the Princess of Detoriola. The SLAG Nation is in agreeance that the balance of power must be restored between both worlds and as such shall empower Lord Soubackalou to travel between the Realm and The Real until such a time as the balance of power is restored to the Real. The SLAG Nation will undergo study to determine the best way to force removal of Princess Nadine's tether and ultimately conclude her travel between both worlds. Until then, Lord Soubackalou has, within this right, the power to bring the balance back as means seem fit. Should Lord Soubackalou attempt to undermine the balance of power in either worlds Lord Soubackalou will be expelled from the Real and face judgement by the SLAG Nation for any violations committed outside the singular objective of balancing power. This is the binding ruling of the SLAG Nation and subject to enforcement as the SLAG Nation see fit.

It would take much cunning and wit from the princess and her companion to stop the efforts of the Dark Lord. The damage caused would leave them all irrevocably changed.

Chapter 1

Nadine

It had been two weeks and there were no signs of my nemesis, just as the family told me there would not be. It had been through a Ouija board in the Real that something had sought me out though, trying to instill fear. The spirit claimed to be Lou, but the family felt it was just a random vicious spirit causing havoc. Danny believed me though or at least he said he did. He had taken a journey to visit a friend who was more knowledgeable on travelling between worlds. He was still away trying to find answers for me, so we had not been in contact. I figured no news was good news after two weeks. I hoped so anyway. Until Danny returned though we would not know for sure. Perhaps it had been a vicious spirit like the others thought. Worst things had happened to me. I was actually, not happy really but possibly, content for it to be something that simple. I really had been praying for something simple after the past year of my life.

During the past year, I had found out that I was not from this world but another one all-together, a world I could only be reached by traveling through the Dreamscape. Not only was I from another world but I was a princess destined to inherit the throne of my kingdom, Detoriola. Being a princess should have rocked, but unfortunately for me, my kingdom was at war with the Dark Lord Soubackalou, who believed he should be the ruler of our kingdom. He had been married to my mother, but his reign had been short-lived due to my mother's apparent suicide. Our kingdom was a matriarch though, the crown passing to the last-born girl of the family. That made me next in line for the throne. I had been sent away in order to protect me from the Dark Lord's wrath. I would have taken the throne long ago had it not been for the loss of my memories and my inability to stop travelling between both worlds. I had been tortured, raped and lost a child to the demented will of Soubackalou, Lou as he liked to be called. Though I had found a way to vanquish him, he used my child to be reborn. Since his return, he had gone into hiding and it had been quiet, too quiet for my liking. The others tried to tell me not to worry but I couldn't help it. I knew it was him reaching out to me via the Ouija board. Somehow, he had found a way to reach out to me from beyond the Realm. It was only a matter of time before he made himself known again.

I was contemplating these very thoughts as I made my way to work. I had been back from the lake house for about a week already and was trying to find a new normal. So many things had happened over the summer, over the last year really, that changed how I saw the world and who I was. Before my return to the Realm, I had been a perpetual victim. First to the sadistic whims of the addict I called my mother, Lily, and her carousel of demented boyfriends. Then when I eventually returned to the Realm to Lou and his nefarious plans. With the help of those around me though, I was able to break past the victim mentality and become stronger. I was closer each day to living up to the standard of the warrior race I was born to. I knew I would never be as powerful a warrior as my sister, Unicorn, but I could hold my own. It still hadn't stopped Lou from raining down terror on my life in the Realm. I shuddered to think what would happen if he found a way into the Real, even if it was only in spirit.

School had begun again as did my sessions with Miss Pauline. She doubled my sessions to twice a week after the events of the past summer. I had found myself in another unexplainable coma for several days while I had been giving birth and losing my child to the Dark Lord. Last thing I needed was more therapy, especially when I could not tell anyone what really happened. I didn't mind though. It was cathartic writing out my issues. I had taken to maintaining two journals keeping my dual lives separate and only letting Miss Pauline read the one about the Real. I journaled about my relationship with Carter and our trust issues. I wrote about my apprehensions joining cheerleading again, especially after the spirit board incident. The cheerleaders thought I was a freak as it was. That was just more icing on the cake. Miss Pauline seemed to understand the pains I was going through. Then again, she only knew the half of it, quite literally.

It had been a long practice that afternoon and I was a bit distracted as I headed to Mr. Fong's. I figured I could get in some solo floor time in before the kids arrived for class. I hadn't realized at first the train I was on was nearly empty. My mind was elsewhere recalling the summer and the turbulent end of it. I was not paying attention to my surroundings, as I had been trained to do, and had not noticed I was nearly all alone on the empty train. When I say nearly alone it was because there were three ragged looking men who all seemed to be focused on me. It wasn't just that the men were ragged. I had seen my share of homeless men in my time, but this was different. They were different. There was something missing inside them. Normal people had a certain look of fullness to them. The bodies and souls of normal human beings were woven together in harmony presenting a look of fullness. These men did not have that same harmony within them though. It looked as if their soul had been ripped from their bodies and what remained was a jagged mis-shaped mess. Their eyes told a hallowing story. They were clear of life rimmed in silver. These men were not human beings anymore. I wasn't sure what they were, but they were not human. Not completely anyway.

I stood cautiously holding my bag loosely. The ragged men were blocking the doors. I would have to go through them to get out. I tried to shake off my rising concern. The energy coming off these creatures was not good or wholesome in anyway though. It was what I felt when I was around demons. It was an unclean feeling that made me want to shower twice over. All I could feel coming off them was malice. They intended to do harm and from the looks of it what they wanted to harm the most was me. I had to get away from them and quickly. I moved just beyond their reach but closer to the doors cautiously. None of the ragged men moved but three sets of eyes were focused solely on my every moment. Something was definitely wrong.

"Hey fellas. Mind if a girl gets by," I said trying to sound calm while being anything but.

One growled at me, actually growled at me. He growled like a feral animal. If that wasn't frightening enough, a single word slipped through his lips sending shivers up my spine. "Princess."

I dropped my bag immediately. The men came at me all at once. I used the bar above my head to catapult them in the opposite direction. I picked up my bag and swung it at the first to recover. It fell back with a grunt. Hands grabbed my arms in efforts to subdue me. I thrusted my elbow back and grabbed its head. I tossed the man into his fallen comrade. Spinning on my heel I thrust out my leg into the third man. He crashed into the window splintering the protective glass. The train pulled into the station and I hurried from the scene slinging my bag over my shoulder.

I didn't look back hurrying away from the station. I needed to get to safety and quickly. I wasn't sure what they were, but I had a sneaky suspicion that Lou had something to do with it. I had to get to the Realm and see what the others could tell me. I made it to my front door thinking I was safe. Instead I found another empty being standing there. Quickly, I ducked out of sight. Luckily for me that it had not seen me. It was turned away from me, looking in my window. Panic sprung up my spine. My grandmother or Sarah could have been home, and those things were at my doorstep. I couldn't let them hurt these two elderly women who meant the most to me in this world. No way.

I dropped my bag readying myself for more hand to hand combat. Thank God for Vega and his hours of training. At that, thank God for Mr. Fong's training as well. I may be powerless in the Real, but I knew how to defend myself. I stood and with determination set in I walked over to the creature pretending to be human on my step.

"Come on. Bring it on, dead eyes," I yelled.

The creature turned to me. I lowered my hands stunned. This fractured being was not filled with malice like the others had been. There was something different about him. This one was fractured but not like the others. This creature had a soul I recognized. I approached slowly and cautiously. It was hard to believe but I recognized him. I was in disbelief, but I could tell who it was I was looking at even though the vessel he was in looked nothing like him. Confused, I approached.

"Danny," I questioned cautiously.

He nodded, holding a finger to his lips. He motioned for me to follow. We rounded the house together to find two more of the dead eyed things in my yard. As soon as they spotted us, we were on them. Danny grabbed a rake bringing it down on the nearest beast. I grabbed the lid of a trashcan and smashed it into the face of the thing. Both beastly men fell back. Scrambling to their feet they came at us again. I took down the dead eyed man before me with ease as I had been trained to do. Danny was having a harder way to go though. Danny had not been trained as a warrior but a scholar. Still, he was doing a fine job at defending himself. The man was slow, and Danny took him down after a few hits. We battled the dead eyed men until they eventually retreated. When the men were no longer in sight, I turned to Danny, taking in the body he was squished into.

I recognized the vessel Danny was in. The blond hair and perfect features belonged to a boy who had been in a coma for the last year after a motorcycle accident, Josh Groves. He was a football star and had been very popular before the accident. He had been drinking one night though and had been run off the road by someone he had been playing chicken with. Last I heard, he was still in a coma. From the look in his blue eyes I would say he still was. The rims around his eyes had the same silver tint as the men I had battled on the train and in my yard. His body had been claimed but fortunately for me it was by someone I knew. It didn't explain to me why though.

"What the hell is going on, Danny," I barked.

"You were right all along. Soubackalou is here in the Real," he told me catching his breath.

I slid into a chair on the patio shocked. What I had dreaded had happened. I had been right. Danny went on to tell me about where he had been the last two weeks.

Danny had gone to visit a friend who was very familiar with travelers and alternate ways into the Real. Vex was an interpreter for the SLAG Nation, the only group known to be able to send individuals at will in between worlds. They actually lived inside the Conduit, a place between the Dreamscape and the Realm. The SLAGs were beings whose appearance was alien like. Their heads were larger than any normal humans. Their appendages were very thin. They were nearly emotionless, craving knowledge above all else, all types of knowledge. They believed themselves above the laws of the Realm. Because of the abilities they had to send individuals into the Real, they were given a wide berth.

As it was, Lou had convinced them that Detoriola had an unfair advantage having such a powerful being as I was with the ability to travel between the two worlds unhindered. He convinced the SLAGs to give him access between worlds as well to balance the power. The SLAGs realized too late though Lou did not just intend for him to be able to travel between worlds but some of his demons as well. It took some great negotiation skills, but Danny was able to convince them to send him as well in order to keep the balance of good and evil. Danny had been elected my guardian as my Uncle Fuller had once been before his passing. Danny didn't even have time to inform Gloria what was happening. He was only able to send word ahead before he was transported into the body of a coma patient suitable to be able to protect me best. Once he was able to get away from the family his vessel belonged to, he had headed right there to find me and tell me what was happening.

"So, let me get this straight. Lou is somewhere in this world with a gaggle of demons at his beck and call hiding in the bodies of coma patients," I recapped.

Danny nodded solemnly.

I shook my head with a sigh before saying, "Damn it! When will you people just listen to me when I warn you guys about something?"

"I am sorry this is happening, Nadine. You are right. The others should have listened to you. When we return this evening, I will tell them all I know. We will come up with a way to fix this. I promise," he swore to me.

I wished I could believe that. I had a sinking feeling that some bad things would happen before Lou was pushed out of that world in a permanent way. I hoped I was wrong but knew deep down that I wasn't. Lou was going to cause havoc in the Real and I was literally powerless to stop him. It was bad enough the things he had done to me in the Realm. I didn't want to fathom the things he could do to the unsuspecting people of the Real. The worst part of it all. I had no idea what his vessel looked like. He could be anyone. Everyone was a suspect.

Chapter 2

By the time I arrived back at the palace, Danny had already explained what was happening to my sister and cousin. The throne room was abuzz with ideas being thrown around on how to fix the situation. Everyone seemed to agree for now Danny would act as my guardian in the Real until the situation was resolved. Not that the SLAGs gave them a choice really, but it was Danny stuck as my guardian for the foreseeable future. I found this laughable since Danny, while formidable as a diplomat, did not have the warrior instincts that my sister or Antonio did. It didn't matter though. The SLAGs were only giving permission to Danny and no one else to follow me into the Real. As much as I was worried about Danny in the Real though, I had larger concerns.

"How do we get the SLAG Nation to pull Lou's access to the Real," I asked the group.

"Negotiating with the SLAGs is not an easy task. They do not understand the ideals we all live by. Love and hate are foreign concepts for them. Revenge is not something they can comprehend easily. We have to find a way to make them see this course of action will provide nothing but a bigger imbalance. It will not be easy at all," my cousin Gloria said.

Gloria was seated on the throne, my throne. She had been elected after her own mother's passing to rule in my place until I was ready. Though I had reached the age required, my swiss cheese memories and the fact I was still tethered to the Real made her reign extend passed the desired time. In all her copper eyed glory, she not only ruled Detoriola but sat upon the Kingdom Council, a group of seven men and woman who enacted the laws for the whole of the Realm.

"I don't care how hard it will be. We need to get him out of the Real at all costs. I will not let him hurt the people I care about there. I – I just can't let that happen," I said feeling the panic set in.

Who knew what Lou was doing as we argued about how to handle the situation. He could be hurting someone I loved, and I had no power to stop him. I was the most power being any of them had seen in the Realm yet powerless to stop Lou from harming anyone in the Real. I was powerless in the Real. I was just an ordinary girl. No, that was not right. I was far from ordinary. My circumstances made me far from ordinary. Still, no one in the Real knew of the Realm or who I truly was. Not only would we have to find Lou but do so without alerting anyone of the truth. The odds were stacked against us in a big way.

"We understand your frustration, Nadine. We truly do. We will do our best to rectify this. Until then, you must be careful. Both of you must be careful. Lou will most likely know someone has been sent to keep you safe. He won't know who though. All your relations in the Real are in danger," Unicorn said.

"Tell me something I don't know," I muttered.

For that I received a scornful look from my sister. I ignored the look though. Had the family listened to me when I told them something was amiss, then we might have been able to stop Lou's plan. Instead, the brushed off my concerns just like they always did. I was really getting tired of it. I was tired of being taken with a grain of salt because of my swiss cheese memories and because I was still just a child to them all. It didn't help I only looked like a teenager when I should really be double in age. My time in the Real was thanks for that.

"Maybe next time you should just listen to me," I said stomping off.

That would get me in trouble later. I didn't care though. The debating was wasting precious time. I had to get back to the Real. I had to protect the people I cared about. I had to be prepared. Most importantly, I had to get Danny prepared.

If Danny was going to be in the Real with me, he would have to be the one getting educated this time around. He needed educating in the ways of the Real. I would be the teacher now and he my student. We had little time to prepare though. School would be coming early the next day and Josh Groves had to be re-enrolled in order for him to stay close to me. A year in a coma put the football star behind. He would be a junior with me, which was ideal. We could tailor his classes to fit my schedule as much as possible. Danny was a brilliant man, but he had no clue of what it was like to be a high school student. Math would not be an issue for him, but he was completely unfamiliar with American history or geography for that matter. His coma would be a good cover for Josh's memory issues. He would have to get up to seep on mannerisms and how to speak first and foremost though. Forgetting who Abraham Lincoln was wouldn't be a problem but forgetting typical American slang would most definitely be an issue.

While not in school, I would get him into better fighting shape. He could join me in my sessions with Vega and Quintus in the Realm. While in the Real, he could accompany me to Mr. Fong's. The children's class I assisted with had grown and Mr. Fong had been hinting at hiring more help. Danny could be an easy fit for the need. On our down time, I could show him some of what I had been learning from the old sensei. We would both need to be in tip fighting shape if we would be going against a number of dead eyed demon possessed.

Somewhere in between all that we would find a way to figure out who Lou was hiding in. He had the advantage since he knew what I looked like already. My vessel in the Real looked exactly like I did in the Realm. That was because I had been born into the vessel unlike the rest of them. I became Nadine Ruth when I was sent into the Real. That was why my soul was evenly captured in my body. Danny and the rest of the possessed had been forced inside the body of those who were no longer inhabiting their bodies. It was why I could see the jagged boundaries around them. It was the only way I was able to tell the difference between a normal person and a possessed. That advantage would not always be available though from what Danny told me.

"Over time, the possessed will settle more into the vessels they are in. The jagged edges will smooth out and it will be near impossible to tell the difference," He informed me.

So, we had to find out who Lou was inhabiting and quickly. Once we figured that out, we had a better shot of figuring out his plans. I was sure he had something insidious planned. I had to stop him before he hurt anyone from the Real. No one deserved to be at the whim of his evilness. I knew this from first-hand experience. Danny and I would figure it out. We had to before things got out of hand.

I also had to figure out something to tell Carter and the rest of my friends. Danny, as Josh Groves, would be spending a lot of time with me. I was not even taking into account the obvious clique difference. Josh had run in a completely different circle of friends than I did. Josh's old friends would not be our biggest problem though. With a believable backstory, we could overcome that obstacle while possibly keeping Josh's life somewhat intact for when he might eventually return. I wasn't even sure if that was really a possibility, but I felt bad thinking any other way. We did, in fact, borrow his body after all. I knew adding Josh to our small group would not sit well with the others, mostly because of my fragile relationship with Carter.

I had spent the summer at my family's lake house hiding from my friends. I knew my body would betray that I was pregnant. I was not pregnant in the Real but in the Realm. My body developed in both worlds though as if I was pregnant in the Real. When my friends surprised me with a visit, they found more than they bargained for with my swelling belly. I lied about my circumstances but after I went into labor the doctor outed my deception. After my latest stint in the hospital, Carter and I had a huge fight. He knew I was lying to him about a lot of things, but he had no idea the depth of what I was keeping from him. I had been ready to give Carter up to save him from a greater heartbreak down the road. No, that's not right. I was not ready to give Carter up and neither was he ready to give me up. Carter had been prepared to sweep all that had happened under the rug and start fresh again. Our Junior year was supposed to be a fresh start but then Lou happened. Now instead of concentrating on what time I had left with my friends in the Real before the family figured out how to break my tether, I had to concentrate on hunting a deranged lunatic. So much for a year of being a normal teenager girl.

<u>Last of the Dream Warriors – Jealousy</u>

I had to figure out a way to have them accept Josh and not be suspicion of the time we spent together. We were a tight knit group who really didn't hang out with anybody outside our little circle, so it was a herculean feat to say the least. Still, it had to be done. Danny needed to be around me so we could protect each other. We would just have to be really convincing. Before all that though we needed to gather the Council in order to formally petition the SLAGs for help. Yeah, can you say doomed?

The Council was a gathering of individuals from all seven kingdoms of the Realm that enforced the laws of the land. I had a sore spot for the Council as it was because of their punishment when I vanquished Lou without permission or in the heat of battle. He had just finished torturing and raping me when I had done it but that didn't seem to matter with the Council. I spent one week stuck in the Real unable to sleep. I almost went crazy with exhaustion and ended up spending an extra week in the hospital because of it. They were not my favorite people, needless to say. Even with Gloria on the Council there were six others all with their own agendas, especially Samurata. Samurata was from the Shadowland where Lou hailed from as well. He had taken great pleasure in my punishment over vanquishing Lou. That was all before Lou decided to use my child as a vessel to return. Now Lou had a totally different vessel there in the Real I had to worry about as well. We still had to figure out what to do with the SLAG Nation and with the Council was the only way to do it.

Gloria was able to gather the Council to petition the SLAG Nation hopefully as a unified front. The other six leaders of the Council arrived in short order. I recognized them all from my return into the Realm as well as when they rendered my punishment. They had all been present and eager to see what I might remember. At the time of my return, it had not been much. I remembered a lot more now though. I remembered it was the Council that had decided to send me into the Real and not the decision of my family. Holding back the identity of Diana's father had been the last straw in a long line of issues I had with the Council. From what had peeked out from my lost memories the Council and I were not friends. After punishing me for vanquishing Lou even less so. We would have to convince them of the immediate need for Lou's removal. This was going to be an uphill battle. I was ready for the challenge though. I had a whole world to protect and not just any world. It was my world and not one was messing with my world.

I walked into the Council chamber to see all six members as well as my cousin sitting at a long marble table elevated away from the people. I stood before the Council as I had many times before in the illuminating light. It was for those typically accused of a crime to spotlight on them. It was where judgement happened, and people usually plead for their lives. That was not the case this time though. This time I was pleading for the lives of those in the Real. The rest of my family standing off to the side and as I waited to be recognized.

Xavier from Genfield raised his hand toward me as he said, "The Council of the Seven Kingdoms acknowledges the Princess of Detoriola."

"Thank you, sir." I needed to be polite if I was going to get their assistance.

Xavier asked, "What is it the Council can do for you, princess?"

Though they knew why I had come before them today, the Council never deviated from their many formalities. This was just one example. Instead of having a meeting of the minds to address the issue, I had to formally bring the issue to court. I had to place it on record. That was their way for over a thousand years. It sickened me I had to play their game to get results. I had no other choice though. I needed the Council.

"I have come to seek assistance and obtain any progress in the removal of the Dark Lord and his minions from of the Real," I stated

Kilgore was the one to respond next, "Any progress with the SLAG Nation is slow going. Just to get an audience with them can take days, if not weeks."

The SLAGs were not known to bow to any authority but their own. Unlike any other being in the Realm, the SLAGs were not subject to the will of the Council. If they did not wish to heed the call, the SLAGs simply ignored the request. An intrigue was typically the only way to get the SLAGs attention. We had to figure out what that intrigue could be in order to gain their audience.

"We are doing what we can to expedite this as quickly as we can. These things take time," Devon of Bock explained.

"Time is something I do not have," I warned them.

Samurata scoffed by saying," I told you all. Unruly as ever."

They had been talking about me. I wasn't sure if that was a good thing or a bad thing. The way Samurata sounded he was not in favor of any resolutions that included me. He was from the Shadowland though, like Lou. I didn't expect him to be in favor of anything that had to do with a Detoriolian vs one of his own. As far as we knew, he was part of Lou's greater agenda. The halfling set my teeth on edge every time I was near him. Samurata' s black eyes and red skin made him a formidable looking individual as it was. I didn't want to tangle with him but the lives of those I loved in the Real were on the line.

"The situation is frustrating to us all. Dear princess, we will do what we can. Every form of government, even that of the Real, goes no faster than it can when dealing with creatures such the SLAGs," Gone from Haasfolk offered.

"I appreciate all the efforts this Council is making on my behalf. It is not my own life I care about but those of the Real. The possessed have attacked civilians in this war the Dark Lord has brought into the Real." I was getting frustrated and when I was frustrated my mouth had a mind of its own.

I was stretching the truth a bit. Yes, Lou's minions had possessed coma patients, but I could not be 100% sure they had hurt anyone. At least not yet. I knew it was only a matter of time though. They were demons after all, and Lou was a sadistic bastard who got off on hurting innocent lives. Having all those unsuspecting people in the Real at his fingertips would be a feast for him. It was like releasing a kid in a candy store and telling him he could have his fill. There was much damage Lou would inflict if he was not stopped.

Samurata laughed as he said, "There is no war. There is only a throne to be rightfully claimed. The throne of Detoriola belongs to the Dark Lord.

This siege of the Real would not be happening if he were granted back what is rightfully his."

"I am sorry, Samurata of the Shadowland, but I beg to differ. The throne belongs to my family. If the Dark Lord wants it, he will have to get it the hard way and fight us on our own territory. Bringing the innocent people of the Real into this only shows he is not only unworthy of the throne but has no honor in him," I told him.

I was baiting the halfling, but he was doing the same to me. This was my kingdom Lou wanted. He had conspired long ago to get it when he married my mother. Detoriola was a matriarch though. Only a female could rise to the throne and at that, the last born to the family. Lou, though married to my mother, never had any claim to the throne. That did not stop him plotting his revenge. He wanted Detoriola. He wanted the power it held more than anything else.

My words did not set too well with Samurata as he then barked," Foolish girl! You should not say such things about your betters."

"Prove him to be my better and I will be silenced. Until then I plan to say anything and everything against the Dark Lord until he stops his campaign against both my worlds," I provoked him even further.

Old Matthew with his clean stark white beard stood. He bellowed raising his hands, "Enough. This is not getting us anywhere. The problems between the princess and the Dark Lord are not why we are here. We are here because of issues in the Real. If the demons are allowed roam the Real, they will hurt innocent civilians much like the princess has stated. This I think we can all agree is the truth of the matter."

Gone conceded, "Without the SLAG Nation, we can do nothing to stop this situation."

Old Matthew slowly lowered his ancient form to sit again before saying, "Then we must work harder at the task at hand. What say you, Gloria?"

Gloria who had been silent until this point said, "I agree. This is not about my cousin or the throne. We must pressure the SLAG Nation into a resolution."

In that moment, I couldn't have loved my cousin anymore. I knew she and I didn't see eye to eye in most things. We both believed though that Lou in the Real was not a benefit for anyone. Our family issues aside, Lou should never have been sent into the Real. Because of his treachery not only was my life and the lives of those in the Real at stake but Danny's life was as well. Danny was my cousin's husband, her soulmate. That was not setting well with her.

"When can I expect this to be over," I asked.

"No resolution will be met today. We can and will try our hardest. Have faith in us, Princess. We will do our best," Xavier told me.

I just hoped it would be in time. I hoped no one ended up dead in the Real because of a war that started in my world. My problems here were going to get someone killed in the Real. If that happened, I was unsure how I would live with myself. This was all my doing and I knew it. Lou would have never set his sights on the Real had it not been for me. I had endangered my friends and family. Whatever happened would be my fault. I would do whatever it took to protect my friends though. If it meant breaking the rules, then so be it. I was tired of following the Council's demanded blindly. They had done me wrong one time too many. If Lou came for me, I would defend myself. Powers or not, I would not be the victim to his demented wrath.

"If my hands are forced, I will protect myself and those I care about. This is not a threat but a promise. I will not let him hurt the people I love," I warned them before walking out of the chamber but directed my loathing at Samurata.

The danger had become a whole lot more real than anything I had faced before. I had been tortured and broken by the demon halfling. I knew the extent of what his twisted mind was capable of. He was in a world not ready for his type of evil and he was not alone. Even with Danny by my side, I was unsure if I could contain such evil. Worst of all, I had no idea whose face that evil was lurking behind. I was powerless in the Real. Danny, though a welcomed companion in this, was nowhere near the warrior I had become. I was still learning myself, but I would continue to learn as much as I could to defend those I loved. I had lost enough to Lou already. I would do everything in my power to ensure no more would die by his hands. I would give my own life to protect the ones I loved. I just hoped it didn't really come to that.

Chapter 3

I was mentally exhausted by the time school was in session only twenty-four hours later. Danny and I had spent the night going over various things he needed to know about in the Real. Our roles as teacher and student had reversed but Danny was a much better student than I ever had been. Danny absorbed the knowledge I gave him easily. His crash course of how to be a teenage boy from the Real took up most the evening. We spent some time in the Dreamscape flitting through the dreams of those from the Real closest to the boy he had inhabited to watch over me, so he could get some kind of point of reference when people spoke to him. He was going in blind to how the Real worked and I was only able to give him the basics. Slang, music, mannerisms. It was all part of how we differed from one world to the other. I hoped I was able to arm him with enough facts so that he could get on with his first day without incident.

We had been lucky. Josh's mother didn't blink an eye when her "son" brought a girl home with him just one day after being in a coma for a year. In fact, she welcomed me in with open arms. I think she was just happy to have her all-star son home finally from the hospital. She barely questioned how I knew him or why I was there. She left us alone right away, which was also good. It was also sad at the same time. Josh spent a year in a coma. He had been a golden boy before the accident. They celebrated his every victory. I remembered running into his parents a number of times after a game happy as could be. He had been on the road to a college scholarship when the accident happened. It was obvious his hopeful career of being a football star had been squashed. From Danny, I learned that even though he was whole, Josh would never be able to play football again. The doctors all agreed his knee injury wouldn't stand such a career path. He was no longer a big football star on the path of greatness. His family barely made an effort to welcome him back after such news. Not that Danny knew who Josh's family were or how they should have reacted but still. If I had been in a coma for a year, I hoped my family would treat me better. Then again, I thought of my family in the Real. I didn't expect much better from them. I brushed it all off though. We had much planning to do still.

The plan was I would meet "Josh" outside Miss Pauline's office first thing in the morning. I volunteered during my morning session with her to help the newly conscious Josh reacclimate to his environment. The story we were portraying was he had lost all his memories of his life before the accident. I understood memory loss better than most because of what had happened to me in the Realm though Miss Pauline did not know anything about that. The plan was to be a guide for an amnesiac Josh through his life. Since we both suffered traumatic events in the last year, Miss Pauline liked the idea of coping together. I was more concerned though about Josh's old click trying to keep us apart. The amnesia excuse would play off well to keep them at bay and me around. So, if one of Josh's old friends tried to engage him, he could act as if he did not know them. In truth, he didn't since it was Danny meeting them and not the real Josh. That was another thing. I had to make sure I only called him "Josh" in front of others and not Danny. I had been slipping that up all day and he made sure to chastise me for it each time.

"Josh please, Nadine. We have to get this right or else all will be unraveled," Danny warned.

He wasn't wrong. I was so nervous about Danny being able to pull off someone from the Real. Even how he chastised me screamed not normal. He was an educated man, there was no doubt. A sullen hormonal high school teenager? Danny had a long way to go and little time to get there.

I planned to take Josh under my wing at school to help him maneuver through the roadblocks. That and to get Danny up to speed so he could help identify and dispatch Lou. I wasn't sure how we were going to do the last part, but we would figure it out. We had to. All other obstacles aside, that was our primary goal. We had to find Lou and force him out of the Real at all costs.

I sat outside Miss Pauline's office waiting anxiously for her to finish her interview with Josh. They had been there for over a half hour and I was beginning to get nervous. As guidance counselor, it was her responsibility to ensure Josh was ready to return back to school. I prayed I had packed Danny with enough information to get passed the ever-keen Miss Pauline. My concerns seemed to have been misplaced though. When they finally emerged, they were both laughing happily. I let out a breath of relief.

"Hello, Miss Ruth. I can say with great pleasure I am happy to give Mr. Groves into your hands. I think you will find him as amusing as I do. Here is his class schedule. Please ensure he makes it to his first class on time," She told me handing me Josh's new schedule.

"I will, Miss Pauline. Thanks."

When Miss Pauline returned back to her office, I looked at Josh a bit surprised. He just shrugged his shoulder saying, "I spend all day being a diplomatic to all manners of creatures. Did you really think I couldn't handle one little schoolteacher?'"

I watched him walk away chuckling at my underestimating him. Danny was right. I was being overly sensitive. His diplomatic background would do him well while in those walls. I was lucky to have him with me instead of some random warrior. I needed someone with a big brain and not just brawn. It would be good to have such an ally beside me in this fight. I just hoped his diplomatic services would not be needed very often. We had a long way to go and a world of possibilities to where Lou could be hiding.

Josh shared several of classes with me as we planned which was good. The more we stuck together the better. He was able to pass off his inability to recognize his former friends easily blaming the coma as we practiced. After the first couple of classes, none of them even bothered to approach him. It was apparent that since he was unable to recall them and more importantly, no longer the star athlete he had been before the accident, that he no longer appealed to his former circle. That would make things a whole lot easier in the long run, but it was unfortunate Josh's friend abandoned him so easily. Josh had lived a fairly shallow life before the accident, and it showed by how many people were still standing by his side after. In his case, not even his family seemed to care he was awake again. It made our job much easier but sad just the same.

The real challenge came when we headed to lunch. I would have to introduce Josh to my friends and Carter. That was the part I hated the most. More lies would be spread between me and my friends. All I felt like I had been doing since returning to the Realm was lie to my friends and each time it did not sit well with me. I had to protect Danny's identity though, more than my own. That first meeting would be very important. They had to believe us if this was going to work. I tried hard to not be nervous but was failing miserably. Danny could see my despair and patted my shoulder.

"It will be fine. Your friends will either accept me or not. Either way, I will be a part of your inner circle. Most importantly, I will be here for you," he said comforting me.

"I am supposed to me consoling you during your introduction to this society not the other way around. Just try to be cool, Danny."

"Josh. It's Josh, remember," Danny corrected me.

I wanted to kick myself. I had to calm down. I was going to mess this up before Danny – Josh - could utter a word to them. I breathed deep and plunged forward, Josh trailing behind me. It was now or never. As much as I wanted it to be never, it had to be done. I was introducing one part of my life to the other. Only one of those worlds knew the truth about me though. My worlds were colliding and there was nothing I could do to stop it. Should be fun, right? Yeah, so not.

Kelly Ann gave me an odd look when we sat down. Sam didn't even bother to look up from the food he was shoveling in his mouth. He usually didn't pay much attention to anything at lunch though except Kelly Ann and the menu, so I was not surprised. Carter was nowhere to be found yet which I counted as a blessing. Kelly Ann motioned silently to my little shadow, Josh. I put on a slight smile and started the tale we created.

"Hey guys. This is Josh. I have been assigned to help him," I informed them.

"To help him with what exactly," Kelly Ann asked looking at him through curious eyes. *Here we go.*

"Oh! Wait a sec! You're Josh Groves. Kels, he's the guy everyone's been talking about. You know the guy who just woke up from being a coma for the past year. Dude, hey," Sam said reaching his hand out to Josh.

Sam accepted Josh completely with no issue or questions. That was why Sam rocked. He didn't judge any one beyond if they were cool with him or not. I wasn't sure if Kelly Ann would be as easy though. One down, two to go.

Josh shook it, happily. "Hey. Thanks for letting me sit with you. It has not been easy trying to figure all this out. I thank the Great Maker for Nadine. She has been heaven sent."

I cringed when he spoke about the Great Maker. While most people would have said God his people in Haasfolk called Him the Great Maker or just Maker in general. It was one of those things I didn't have a chance to go over with him before all this happened. The others didn't flinch though much to my surprise. They had lots of questions for him. Instant celebrity status. We were all listening to Josh regale us on the ins and outs of relearning how to button jeans when Carter approached. I felt him before I saw him. I could feel the waves of confusion coming off him even before he reached the table. He didn't speak though. Instead, he stared at Josh sitting beside me and he did not look happy.

"Hey Cartman. Did you meet Josh yet? Dude, he just spent a year in a coma. Isn't that some shit," Sam told him.

Carter didn't respond. He just looked at me with one question in his head. I knew what he wanted to ask me. Why was Josh here? He wanted to know more importantly, what was Josh to me? The true answers, I could never tell him. I couldn't tell him that Danny was my cousin's husband. I also didn't want to lie. I had been lying to him about so much and our relationship had suffered for it. As much as I wanted to tell him the truth, tell all my friends the truth I was bound. I was bound by the Council and my own fears.

I lowered my head instead continuing with my lunch. Carter without even saying a word to me or Josh decided he didn't want to sit with us that afternoon. He made his decision about Josh without uttering a single word to him. Carter told Sam he would see him later before heading out of the lunchroom. That was the meeting I dreaded, and it went exactly how I expected. Kelly ann said it best though.

"Boys. Can't believe for one second a girl can just be friends with a guy," Kelly Ann mused.

No truer words were spoken.

"Hey, don't harsh on my man. He is just protective of what's his," Sam grumbled.

Thus, began a great debate between Kelly Ann and Sam on women, men and property rights. As they bantered back and forth Josh and I were not listening. Josh was looking at me curiously. I tried not to pay attention, but he was being obvious.

"What," I asked in a whisper.

"That young man has claim you as his mate," Josh asked sincerely.

I knew what he was thinking. I wasn't sure how I could explain my relationship with Carter. He was more than a boyfriend. Was he my mate though? In these terms, people from the Realm would agree he was my mate. It also meant many in our junior class were mated, multiple times. Our relationship was not as simple as being mates. I definitely could not explain it to him in front of the others. I would give him a break down of how relationships in the Real worked later. That was as soon as I figured out how they all worked myself. For now, I had to let him know the conversation was to be tabled.

"Things work differently here, Josh. Not everything is as black or white as you may think it is," I whispered.

<u>Last of the Dream Warriors – Jealousy</u>

"That boy thinks you are his mate, Nadine. He sees me as a threat. That is as black and white as you can get," Josh stated firmly.

I couldn't lie to him. What he said was the honest truth. Carter saw Josh as a threat to our already rocky relationship. It didn't matter that we were just sitting innocently having lunch together with the rest of our friends. Carter saw Josh as a problem. It was going to take a lot more convincing to change his mind, if at all. It would not bode well for our mission if Carter got too suspicious of Josh. I would have to convince him somehow Josh was not the enemy without compromising his identity or even worse my own. It should have been simple adding a friend to our circle, but I had to be in love with a hothead.

It definitely would not be easy, especially since we were still on rocky terms after my latest stay in the hospital. In the Realm, I had given birth to a child Lou used to bring himself back to life. None of this was known to Carter though. I had lied to Carter and my friends telling them I had a rare condition. The doctor looking after me outed my lie and Carter had not taken it well. He had no proof I was actually pregnant since my body in the Real did not carry the child, but he knew I had been lying. What I was lying about had not been clear to him though. Between the loss of my child and a very dear friend I had not been myself. I had pushed him away and with good reason. Those reasons though were not enough to keep us apart. My eventual end in the Real was not enough to keep us apart. I needed Carter and he professed the same need. Still, our relationship had taken a big hit because of my double life. We were just getting back to some semblance of normal again when Lou pierced the veil between our worlds. I had to figure out how to make Carter believe Josh was just someone who needed my help. It would not be easy but lately nothing seemed to be.

After spending the afternoon showing Josh around school and introducing him to Mr. Fong, I found myself at home alone. I was exhausted after explaining how relationships evolved in the Real, especially for teenagers. Despite my explanation, Danny still thought Carter believed me to be his mate. I stopped arguing and left him at his house shortly after. Josh's family wanted some time alone with him and I needed to get home to mine. I forgot Gillian and Sarah were spending the evening in bible study which meant I had the house to myself. I was surprised when there was a knock at my door when I was getting ready for bed. I had just wrapped up my homework for the evening. Cautiously, I answered and found Carter there.

"Hey," He whispered not looking at me.

I looked at him for a moment before letting him in. He sat still unable to look at me. I stood in front of him, hands on hips. God, he was so frustrating. I know I had been lying to him, but as far as this world was concerned everything, I had told them was plausible. He wasn't mad at me for any of my omissions though. He had been mad about another boy sitting next to me at lunch. It was so juvenile and frankly petty.

"Why were you such a jerk to Josh today," I asked already knowing the real answer.

"Why was he sitting with you," Carter countered.

"The guy just woke up from a coma and doesn't remember a soul. I was trying to be nice. I was hoping my boyfriend could have been nice to him too. He is a nice guy after all."

"I am sure he was nice. All guys are nice until they get what they want," he muttered.

I grabbed his chin and forced him to look at me as I said, "There is nothing going on with Josh and me. There never will be something going on between Josh and me. I am not a possession, Carter Alan James. Grow up and stop treating me like a toy."

Yeah, I went there. I three named him. He had it coming after all for being a bonehead.

Carter gripped my hips looking up at me after I released his face. He smiled mischievously as he said, "But you are my favorite thing I love to play with."

He pulled me onto his lap with a squeal. I smacked his shoulder but stayed right where I was. He had been a jerk, but he was my jerk. Not to mention, I had been missing his warmth all day. Perhaps Danny had been right. Perhaps Carter was my mate. I couldn't see me feeling like that with anyone but him. I kissed him fiercely. He had to hold me tightly so I would not fall off his lap.

"Don't ever doubt my feelings for you," I told him.

"Same," he told me before kissing me again.

Even if Carter was not my mate, he was something more for me than just a boyfriend. He had my heart. Whatever was to come I could always count on that.

Chapter 4

Soubackalou

I stretched, flexing my newly acquired muscles. This puss bag was out of shape, but I could change that with some time and effort. After all, the vessel given to me had been in a coma for the last ten years. What was I expecting, perfection? The body was just a means to an end, temporary. Still, I wanted my temporary housing to fit enough to let me do the things I needed. It wasn't a perfect fit, but it would do for what I needed it for. It came with excellent credentials and lots of possibilities. I so enjoyed the possibilities it would help me create.

"While we have no current openings for a full-time position, I can assure you we are always looking for talent. If something comes open in the meantime, we would like to keep you on our roster for subbing for now," the nasally other bag of puss sitting before me said.

I had nearly forgot he was there. It was what boiled my demon blood, having to deal with parasites like the weasel of a man they called principal. I needed access to the school in order to ferret out my prey. The predator in me needed to hunt but there was one of the roadblocks I was forced to deal with in this world. Still, if all that was keeping me from my hunt was a fragile thing like him then I would have the princess in my grasp in no time. I had some fun ahead of me any way I looked at it. I just had to play by their rules, for now anyway.

"Of course. You have my information should a position open up. I am readily available to you and this fine institution," I said with my impressively deceiving smile.

Last of the Dream Warriors – Jealousy

I left the office with a plan hatching even before I made it to the street. I just needed to figure out which little piggy would not make it to market that evening. Since I was still getting used to my vessel, I would have to settle for a quick fix instead of a marathon. I looked about searching for my prey. I would bath in their blood and feast on their organs. Why not? I was surprised more of these unsuspecting humans had not turned to cannibalism already with the price they placed on sustenance there. It would save me in the long run. Which little piggy would it be? I needed to choose and soon. I hungered from more than blood lust. The vessel had a hankering for flesh. It craved flesh more than I thought possible. That matched my needs nicely. I knew I would like this vessel. It was such a vicious creature, so much like me. We would have fun together. I was sure of it.

I met Josh at the fountain as planned the next day. Kelly Ann And Sam were already there discussing their schedules. While Sam was more dedicated to classes that focused on manual labor, Kelly Ann's schedule was littered with more finer arts. She was a fabulous artist despite what she told others. The great divide in interests meant they only had a couple classes together. That was not sitting well with Kelly ann. Sam seemed indifferent about the issue. He was the type of guy who didn't need to be with his woman every moment of the day to know she loved him. He didn't get jealous if she talked to another guy. He was confident in his relationship with her. I found myself wishing Carter had such confidence in our relationship. Then again, I hadn't given him much reason to feel confident in us. I lied and kept secrets from him all the time. He had a right to be suspicious of me. I just wished he could trust my love for him like Sam did with Kelly Ann. The rest shouldn't matter.

Josh stood when he saw me approach. He gathered his things and was by my side quickly. "I took the time this morning to review the layout of the school."

"Why," I asked confused.

"If the Dark Lord tries to take the fight to us on campus, I wanted to be familiar with all the areas he could best use to corner us with his minions."

I nodded, in approval. Danny was surprisingly good at this. I would have to mention his strategic abilities to my cousin. Not that she would listen or do anything about it but in the thick of things Danny's abilities may be of use.

I felt two arms wrap around me pulling me back. Fear set in since my senses were on high alert because of Lou. Before I could react though, I felt lips on my own. I relaxed immediately against Carter. It didn't matter that I knew he was proclaiming his position with me by kissing me in front of Josh. It felt good to have his hands on me. It felt good to be so wanted. Sure, he was being a jealous fool for no reason. If it meant I got more welcomes like that I was okay with it, for now anyway.

"So, what are we talking about," Carter asked with his arms still nestled around me.

Josh looked at Carter then to me. He blew out a long breath before stuffing the map in his bag and heading into the school. I knew he was mad I let Carter interrupt his debriefing, but I would deal with him later. I knew my time with Carter would be short since I had to work at Mr. Fong's that evening. Josh would be with me at Mr. Fong's and that meant Carter would not be. I wanted to spend what I could with Carter and school was a safe place as far as I was concerned. Lou would be insane to attack us there. He would be crazy to attack anyone here at all.

"Coma boy is not too happy I stole your attention from him," Carter mused.

I rolled my eyes turning to him and I said, "I am not a toy on the playground, remember? You will both have to share me."

"We may have a problem then because I don't like to share," he said whispering in my ear.

His voice tickled me, sending shivers down my spine and straight to my lady parts. We were at school which was a good thing. Neither of us would let anything happen on school grounds. I laid a gentle hand on his chest giving him a tiny smile. As much as I liked his lighthearted nature, I had to make sure he understood what I needed from him when it came to Josh. He needed to understand Josh was not going away, at least any time soon.

"I need you to be nice to Josh. Please, for me," I begged.

Carter let out a long sigh before saying, "I will try to be nice to Coma Boy for you."

"His name is Josh," I scolded.

"Fine. Josh," he grumbled.

I kissed him happily on the cheek before taking his hand. We headed into school together and despite the looming threat of Lou, I felt better about things than I had in a while. Carter agreed to give Josh a chance. It was more than I could ask for. I needed all of it to work out. Carter meant so much to me and as dysfunctional as our relationship had been, I loved him. I needed him more than I cared to admit. After the dramatic summer I knew time might be short for us. I had to make things work for us. There was no other choice. If I learnt anything from Miriam and Stanley, I knew I needed to fight for the ones I loved. Carter was first and foremost on that list. I could not let Lou get in the way of that. I hated having to lie even more to Carter though. At least, I had someone in that world that I could talk to about everything that was happening to me now. It may not be perfect, but it was close to it. We just had to find Lou quickly so that our perfect bubble would not be broken by his evil deeds.

Chapter 5

Soubackalou

I stood in the middle of the bedroom admiring the lovely shade of red that stained my skin. It was more black than red but either way it looked lovely on my naked body. The fine auburn hairs on my chest matted by the sweat the vessel had exuded as I did what I knew best, torture and mayhem. Who needed clothes when you could wear the blood of innocence? Alas, I found it highly unlikely the masses of meat bags in that world would find my idea of attire fitting. I would have to wash away all this beautiful suffering if I planned to start my day educating the little monsters I was now assigned. With a heavy sigh, I stepped over the lifeless body of the random stray I had picked up on the way home from my evening shopping and headed to the shower.

I smiled at the frightened whimpers of the naked female zip tied to the toilet. Her body was also covered in lovely shades of red but that was mostly from me painting her before I did so many terrible things to her. It had been an exquisite evening to tell it correctly. Even though my erection was still sitting at half-mast I had to ignore my baser instincts. I had my position calling me and my devious plans to continue.

I patted her head gently before whispering in her ear, "I can't right now, my darling pet. I have so many little minds to corrupt. Never fear though. I will be home soon enough, and we can see how much I can make you scream then."

She cringed away from me in fear. I gripped her blood-soaked hair kissing her mouth roughly. She shrieked straining against her restraints. A soft cry left her lips as I let her go. Tears streamed down her cheeks smearing the lovely red. I sighed feeling content as I stepped into the shower. So many minds to corrupt indeed. There were hundreds of unwitting helpers just waiting for someone like me to teach them how to be evil. It was going to be so much fun.

Nadine

It had been a quiet evening on the fields. We were just finishing up sparring when it happened. Vega was stretching out his limbs from a good session. He and Quintus were joking about how shiny Quintus was making the sword he was buffing. It was all good-natured ribbing and a welcomed break from the worrying I had been doing. I saw Vega look passed me and smiled. He stood and moved passed me quickly, very excited. I turned to see him embrace another man. They clasped arms and my mouth gaped open when I saw who it was. I hadn't seen him since the night I was taken by Lou. He had been on my mind on occasion since then, but I had pushed him back down because of what had happened that night. It felt like a lifetime ago but there he was in his leather wear. I thought for the briefest moment I saw a flash of a memory of another time and place but that couldn't be. We never met before my sister's wedding. The flash was something much older than that. I brushed it off quickly.

"AJ," I breathed.

Both men turned to me acknowledging my presence. I could see his devilish grin when AJ saw it was me. He gave me a slight bow, mischief in his eyes. "Good day, Princess."

I still cringed when someone called me princess, especially in that tone. The once beloved term of affection utilized by my uncle had been tainted by Lou and what he did to me. As he had brutalized me in every way he could imagine, the entire time he whispered in his mocking tone that word. I had a physical reaction every time someone called me by my title. I hated it more than anything anyone ever called me.

"Don't call me that," I told him firmly after Vega moved back to stretching giving us our space.

"What shall I call you then, huh? Do you prefer your majesty? Her royal highness perhaps," he asked being a bit snarky.

"Master would do," I played along. The chill I had felt from being called Princess all but forgotten.

"Oh, sweetie you can't master anything much less this," he chuckled as he fluffed himself up.

"You don't know a thing about me. Ask around. I am a lot stronger, powerful, than I look," I told him, intending to brag.

He moved in closer to me invading my personal space. He wanted to intimidate me, and I won't lie, it was working. AJ was formidable. He stood at least an inch over me and he was all muscle under his leathers. His dark features lent to the bad boy persona he was going for. His former faux mohawk was gone now replaced with a short military cut. He smelled all woodsy and very much the man I was sure he was. I was intimidated and he knew it.

AJ smiled knowing he was getting to me before moving back out of my comfort zone. "I was planning on doing a bit of sparring but now I am thinking against it. You wouldn't want to go do something, would you," he asked.

I should have been reporting to Riley for my power lessons. I should have been taking more princess lessons with Danny or teaching him how to be a teenager from the Real. I should have been doing a thousand different things but in that moment all I wanted to do was spend more time with AJ. I didn't know what it was about him, but the rest of the Realm seemed to slip away while I was with him. I felt drawn to him and I couldn't explain it. It made me uncomfortable since I was in love with Carter. Still, AJ drew me in, and I couldn't help myself.

I nodded and asked biting my lip, "What do you have in mind?"

He leaned closer again smiling as he said, "That would ruin the surprise."

AJ held out his hand and I hesitated before taking it. I knew taking his hand was walking over a line in the sand my sister and his brother had made even before their wedding. They had come to us both warning us away from each other. The reaction had produced the opposite effect.

We were off before another word could be said. AJ liked to talk I found out in short order. I found what he was saying more of an education than sitting in the palace pouring over pages with Danny. I loved Danny but if it could not be found in a book, he really didn't care. AJ though was a spirit of his own. AJ told me about his life in January keeping away from the subject of his family oddly enough. He talked about the gypsies and the parties they had. Parties that went on for days, weeks sometimes. They were a proud and happy people who lived for life that did not subscribe themselves to the laws of the land. They didn't belong to just one kingdom but all the seven kingdoms though January was as close as they ever come to having a permanent settlement. While the gypsies believed in some of the same things most creatures of the Realm did, they had a lot less strict list of codes they lived by.

AJ had been living with some relatives who were honest to goodness gypsies for some time, much to Antonio's bemusement. It seemed to be the underlining issue between the two brothers. Every time Antonio had mentioned AJ or their gypsy relatives, which was not very often, he would note his disappointment in the whole lot of them. It was the lifestyle AJ had chosen though and Antonio had no say in his brother's choices. AJ had been growing tired of the endless party though and was looking for something new. He had come back to Detoriola to see what possibilities held for him there.

AJ took me through the Dreamscape to a place he claimed was his own. It looked like any normal home you could find in any suburban neighborhood. The grass was neatly cut and the small fountain in front of the house had real running water. I found this out of character for such a free spirit to want solid four walls to hold him in. What also felt odd was there was not a soul to be found though in this Dreamscape. We were utterly alone which made sense after he told me why. AJ was able to control that Conduit with the power of a dream weaver crystal. He explained to me how he was given it by a young weaver he had once saved from certain death.

"She was under attack by some pretty nasty halflings. Poor thing didn't have a clue how to protect herself. I dispatched the demons in short order, and she rewarded me with this crystal," he told me.

"She did, huh? Did she reward you with just the crystal I wonder," I joked but curious just the same.

"Jealous much," he countered.

I scoffed saying, "Not likely. I have a boyfriend."

He looked me over curiously before shrugging his shoulder and saying, "Can't say I am surprised, but I am curious. Does your family know about this guy? I know the high born all have these things arraigned from birth. Did you at least get to pick the guy or was he chosen for you?"

I narrowed my eyes at him. All of the perceived notions about arraigned marriages was barbaric as far as I was concerned. I knew Gloria and Danny's marriage had been arraigned but they had fell in love before taking vows. Still, it had been an arrangement like AJ was suggesting. Had they not found themselves compatible or at the very least liked each other the wedding would not have proceeded. The same for my sister and his brother. Antonio and Unicorn truly loved each other. While the matches were arranged love was what lead to the marriages, not the arrangement per se.

"Carter is from the Real and he was one hundred percent my choice," I informed him.

My response surprised him. I knew he most likely had heard about my tether to the Real. It was common knowledge by now. Other than Danny though, who had been experiencing the Real first-hand with me, no one really understood what it was like there. Most people in the Realm thought those from the Real were uncivilized and wild beings. They were not completely wrong if they judged the people in the Real by Realm standards. Still, there was so much more to them than people knew. The people from the Real were so much more than uncivilized, untrained vessels. They had heart and strength that could match any seasoned warrior.

AJ quickly recovered folding his arms across his chest by saying, "Well, aren't you the little rebel? I guess the stories about you are all true then, huh?"

That made me angry. I wasn't sure why I was letting AJ goad me, but I was, and it pissed me off. "I don't know what you heard about me and I don't care. My life is not up for speculation like some believe. I may be heir to the throne, but I am still a human being and deserve to be treated as such. If that makes me a rebel then so be it," I said before throwing my hands up in the air.

I began to walk away but AJ grabbed my arm. I looked at his hand on my arm before I looked as his face angrily. My fists were balled, and I was hot with rage. He dropped his grip and backed up, both hands held up in surrender. "Chill. I was just joking."

I saw from the reflection in a nearby window my eyes had a soft blue glow to them. I blinked hard taking a deep breath. I hadn't meant to call upon my power but sometimes it still activated when I got angry. I wasn't able to control how it manifested when that happened. AJ was developing a knack for making me angry. When I looked again my eyes were back to their normal copper color. I turned away from him again breathing deeply.

"I'm sorry. I am still learning how to control it," I told him feeling embarrassed.

He came to me slowly, laying two light hands on my shoulders. I turned to him feeling horrible. I hadn't done anything wrong, but I still felt bad. Had my powers gotten away from me like it almost had when sparring with Unicorn, I could have hurt him. I could have hurt her. I didn't want to hurt anyone. I just wanted to be normal. The only one who truly deserved my wrath was Lou. He was the only one I really wanted to hurt. He was the only one who really deserved it.

"Hey. It's okay. I was being an ass. It would serve me right if you barbequed me," he said trying to get me to smile.

I couldn't resist his smile. It was infection. My lips pulled back in a slight smile. "I wouldn't barbeque you. I wouldn't want to explain to Antonio what I did and why."

"Yeah. He probably wouldn't have blamed you though. I mean, he might actually miss me. Maybe a little. Probably be more a relief than anything. He might actually thank you if you did," AJ smirked.

He ran his hands down my arms trying to comfort me. He was a comfort. It was a comfort I had only knew one other place before. I didn't want to think about that right then though. I wanted to be here in the moment with AJ. Something about him felt right. I craved that feeling more than I should. He made me feel like there was more in the world than pain and misery. He was a breath of fresh air that I didn't realize I needed.

"Thanks, AJ. The others are wrong about you, you know. You are so much more than the bad boy the others believe you to be. You're a great guy," I told him.

He didn't respond to my compliment. Instead, something in his playful eyes changed. They grew cold and unreadable. His fingers gripped my arms firmly. Before I could react, he was pulling me close to him. His lips overtook mine, devouring me. I was consumed by his kiss. I melted against him. His fingers dug into my hair deepening the kiss more. Something inside me broke. His passion for life, for me, made me want more than just a simple kiss from him. My hand ran across his ribs gripping him closer to me just as his hands began to explore me as well. His lips traced my jaw and I moaned feeling a fire ignite in my belly. His lips found mine again, capturing me once more. I didn't want him to stop. I wanted more than a simple kiss. I wanted the freedom it promised.

It was more than a simple kiss though. It was a betrayal. I betrayed Carter, who was a million miles and a world away. It was that realization that broke the spell we were under. Placing both hands against his chest I pushed trying to distance myself from AJ. He was like a rock though, unmovable, as he held me against him. My body began to panic remembering other times I was in such a position of unwanted affections. I remembered Bart trying to kiss me and Lou's unwanted touches. All those horrible unwanted memories flooded me, and I panicked. I pushed against AJ again, this time power came rushing from me. AJ was rocketed away from me landing several feet away.

He quickly regained himself sitting up with a chuckle. "Feisty, aren't you?"

My hands covered my mouth in shock before saying, "Oh god."

I turned on my heels and left the Dreamscape despite him calling for me to come back. I had let AJ kiss me and did nothing to stop him. I let him because I wanted him to do it more than I cared to admit. It was brief and didn't last long but that was because the guilt had been overwhelming. AJ had been too overwhelming. He was all jokes and passion. He was dangerous and I could not let myself be around him again. He had made me forget who I was for a brief moment. I couldn't let that happen again. There was so much going on that I could not forget who I was and what I needed to do. Most of all, I couldn't betray Carter again. He was a world away, but still my boyfriend. Carter was the love of my life. I loved him with everything in me. Somehow though, AJ negated how I felt for Carter. I loved Carter. What confused me though was if Carter was the love of my life, why did I feel such attraction to AJ? Why didn't I stop AJ's kiss sooner? What was wrong with me?

I tried to push back down the confusion and guilt when I headed back into the Real. It was hard but I had convinced myself that what happened with AJ was only a one-time occurrence. I probably wouldn't see AJ again. He was a gypsy by nature and compound with the fact I had tossed him pretty good with my powers, it was a good possibility he was already heading for the border back to his gypsy clan. Besides, it didn't matter in the Real because it happened in a completely different world Carter did not even know about. I knew I was being ridiculous, but it was like the tree falling in the woods' theory. If you weren't there to see the tree fall, did it make a noise? If Carter didn't know AJ and the Realm existed, was it really a betrayal? I wanted it to be as if it never happened so much that I clung to that weak justification. While in the Real I could pretend that all I wanted. AJ didn't exist there, and I was safe from whatever it was I felt for him. I just prayed when I returned to the Realm that AJ really did leave again, this time for good. Unicorn and Antonio had been right. AJ was nothing but trouble.

<u>Last of the Dream Warriors – Jealousy</u>

Danny knew right away something was amiss when he saw me. I was distracted and not just by the looming threat of Lou, which I should have been thinking about. I had not seen Danny at all since the previous day. I had skipped my lessons with him and Riley to spend time with AJ which meant I had not seen him at all in the Realm the night before. Danny didn't know I had seen AJ or why I skipped our lesson. I approached feeling apprehensive and waited for a proper scolding.

"Where were you last night? I thought we had a study session," He asked.

I wasn't sure if I should lie to Danny or not. He was very understanding but what happened could go beyond the bounds of our friendship. He actually knew Carter. Even though they did not get along, I was not sure he would side with me in the issue. Still, Vega and Quintus had been there when I went off with AJ. While I knew Vega would most likely not say anything, I was unsure about Quintus. I wasn't sure about a lot of things. I didn't like lying to Danny though and I needed a sound board. He had always good for that.

"I was hanging out with AJ," I told him.

"AJ? You mean Antonio's kin," He asked confused.

I nodded biting my lip nervously.

"I didn't even know he was back in the area. I didn't even know you knew him like that. Did he say why he is back in Detoriola? How is he doing," Danny asked.

Danny was always quizzical. It didn't surprise me no one knew AJ had returned. AJ was the type to stay under the radar of the family. Since his brother was married to my sister though, that meant he was always welcomed at the palace. It did surprise me he sought out the training fields and not the palace first in his return though. He was familiar with Vega, but it didn't look like he had been there to see him in particular. Had AJ come looking for me? I wasn't ready to voice that theory.

I shrugged before saying, "Not sure but well we kinda had a blow-out."

"Really? What happened," Danny inquired surprised.

I blew out a breath. Here goes nothing. "I tossed him using my powers."

"Why?"

"Because he kissed me."

Danny sat back shocked. He knew my history. He knew what had happened to me with Lou and what Bart had tried to do to me. I had held nothing back form Danny about any of those occurrences. He had been a good friend to me when all that ugliness had gone down. In the Realm, I considered Danny my best friend as it were. So, for him to hear AJ kissed me I knew it would be a shock for him. I had never mentioned AJ or any sort of an attraction before that moment.

Danny looked around. We were alone still since it was so early but at any moment someone might venture upon us. One of those people might be Carter. Still Danny could see I was in need of a friend. He stood up putting his hand on my shoulder looking concerned.

"Are you okay," Danny asked seriously.

I nodded biting my lip again.

"I am so sorry, Nadine. When we get back home I will talk to Gloria. We will get him removed from court immediately, so you won't have to see him again," Danny said trying to comfort me.

I looked at him surprised as I said, "Why would you do that?"

"He tried to force himself on you and you defended yourself. Why wouldn't I?"

Danny had it all wrong. He had it so wrong. He thought I was upset about AJ kissing me. Sure, I was upset about that but for all the wrong reasons. I was upset because I had let AJ kiss me. I had wanted him to kiss me. I was upset that I had wanted it. Danny had to know the truth. I couldn't let him take AJ from me. I couldn't explain it, but I really didn't want him to be banished because of me.

"He didn't assault me, Danny. I let him kiss me," I admitted.

Danny stood there confused. I wanted to explain but didn't get the chance. Carter had approached and wrapped his arm around me. He looked at the confused form of Josh and wrinkled his nose before kissing my cheek. Carter turned facing just me.

"Hey, baby. Morning…Coma boy," Carter greeted us.

I looked from Josh to Carter giving him a harsh look. He shrugged and kissed me again. Josh couldn't look at me. My revelation had the gears in his mind working on overtime. I knew he had so many more questions but couldn't ask them with Carter so near. Instead, Josh wished us a good day and headed inside, my revelation weighing on him as It had me. Carter was oblivious of all this though. He held me close and I gave him a scolding look.

"I asked you to be nice," I reminded him.

"I said morning to him. What more do you want," he grinned trying to be cute.

I huffed out a breath. As frustrating as Carter could be at times, my behavior in the last twenty-four hours had been worse. I would let him slide on the coma boy thing, at least for the day. I didn't want to fight with Carter. Instead, I wanted for him to hold me and take away the bad feelings I was having. I just wanted him to hold me and the world disappear.

Carter could tell I was in another world. He put his arms around me and asked, "You okay, babe?"

"Do we really have to go in today? Can't we just run away and forget the world," I asked curling against him craving his warmth.

"I have no problem skipping reality for the day. Whatever you want to do or wherever you want to go we will," he told me.

I sighed against his chest. I was where I wanted to be, right against him. I looked back at the school and wished I was more spontaneous. I wished for once I wasn't this responsible person. I wanted to be more than the reliable one. Most of all, I wanted a day away from all the other world drama. Perhaps AJ was rubbing off on me in the brief time we had been together but for the second time in less than a day I was going to play hooky. This time though, it was would be with the man I loved.

"I don't care. Let's just get out of here," I begged him.

He kissed my lips lightly before grabbing my hand saying, "You don't have to ask me twice."

We hurried away from school laughing happily. I wasn't sure where we were going when we got in Carter's latest borrowed car from his father's lot, but I didn't care. I leaned against him as he drove and couldn't think of any place I would rather be. We found ourselves at a park on the other side of town. It was empty, which suited us fine. We made out on a bench facing the nearby pond. It was a cloudy day but a nice fall breezy had set upon us. It was a good thing too because kissing Carter always made me hot with need. When our kissing was becoming too intense for both of us, we took a break. Carter pushed me on the swings for a little while instead. I let my head fall back and enjoyed the warm sun on my face as I flew through the air. I felt good, free, to be here with him. I hadn't felt this free in a long time if ever. I wished I could stay there with Carter and pretend the rest of the world didn't exist. I wished I could pretend the psycho trying to kill me wasn't real. I wished I could just be Nadine, girl in love with her best friend. The dark cloud hanging over my head was there though and very real.

After the day began to grow long, Carter and I laid on the grass watching the clouds roll by and talked about our dreams and aspirations in life. Carter didn't want to go into the family business. He was in no way the salesman his father was and had no desire to sell used cars. It was a nice perk to drive any car on the lot, but he didn't have any ambition to sell them. Instead, he dreamed of one day being a reporter or even perhaps an investigative journalist. He wanted others enthralled by what he had to say. He wasn't sure in what venue yet though. Carter had the personality to do it either way. He was always so curious about everything. It was what made it hard keeping all my secrets from him especially in the past year. He was an energetic person though and I knew he could do whatever he set his mind to. I just hoped it wasn't trying to figure out my hidden world.

We talked about my creative writing class I had taken over the summer and my hopes to possibly one day write. I wasn't even sure I would be able to write professionally. It wasn't that I didn't have the talent. I was unsure how long I would be tethered to the Real. My destiny in the Realm had a very different occupation already planned out for me. I couldn't tell him any of that though. Instead, I pretended I was a normal teenage girl recounting my dreams to my boyfriend. Our dreams aligned much to my surprise. We aspired to entertain the masses, me with my writing and Carter with his reporting. We were a match in more ways than even I had realized. Still, the cloud over my head remained. It remained because as well matched as we were there was an invisible wall between us because of all the lies and things I had been keeping from him.

Children of all ages began filling the park, ending our private paradise. It had been a beautiful day though. I didn't want to leave but I had to get to work. Reality was calling us back. Still, I didn't want to go. When Carter said we should leave, I straddled his lap and kissed him as if it was our last kiss. I knew once we left this park our time together would be shortened as Danny and I sought to find Lou. Lou already had been in the Real for at least a week. There was no telling what damage he already had created. We needed to really dig in on our search if we were going to find him. Something else laid heavy on me. I couldn't help but feel once we left that park things would change for us and not in a good way. I wanted to hold on to him and never let go. I feared if I let him go, he would be gone forever.

"I need you," I told him trying to convey this feeling as I held his face in my hands before I kissed him again deeply.

When we broke our kiss, he smiled and said, "If you can't tell I really need you too."

He motioned between us to his bulging jeans. I shook my head, smacking him lightly. He chuckled hugging me against him. We kissed several more times before it was apparent that we needed to leave. If not, the entire park would get a show not suitable for children and neither of us wanted that kind of attention. Carter drove me begrudgingly to work giving me a long lingering kiss before I got out of the car.

"Are you really sure you need to go into work tonight," he asked, hanging out his window with a smile.

I kissed him one last time before I turned on my heels and headed inside before I changed my mind. I blew him one last kiss before making my way through the doors. I didn't want to head back to reality, but I made a commitment with Mr. Fong I had to honor. As tempting as Carter had been all day, there was still something holding me back from taking that next step with him. It was not that I was afraid about the next step. I wanted to be with Carter in every sense of the word. Something seemed to always be in the way though. That evening was no different. Still, I knew he loved me and because of that he would wait until it was the right time. I knew when the time was right, it would be glorious between us. It could be no other way when you were this in love with your partner.

In my euphoric state, I was caught off guard by a very angry Danny. He gripped my arm the moment I entered the building and dragged me into Mr. Fong's office. I was barely able to get a word out since it happened so suddenly. We were already in the office by the time I gathered my bearings. Danny slammed the door behind us finally releasing me.

"What the hell, Danny," I barked rubbing my arm where had had grabbed me.

"You drop a major bomb on me about AJ and then disappear all day long. Do you know how worried I have been all day? When I couldn't find you after homeroom all I could think was the worse. Did you forget that the Dark Lord is still out there hunting you? Did you forget he is out there doing Maker knows what to the inhabitants of this world," Danny yelled at me.

I was taken aback. I never saw Danny get angry before. Sure, he seemed concerned or even stern but never angry. He was always the pinnacle of calm and reason. Danny was furious at me though and for good reason. He was right, of course. I had shirked my responsibilities for a day of childish fun with Carter. I had wanted a day as a normal teenager but neglected the fact that I was anything but normal. Lou was still out there. We were not anywhere closer to identifying his vessel or what the Dark Lord had planned for this world or me. Danny had every right to be angry with me. I did have every right to a day off regardless of what anyone thought though. I had needed the day with Carter more than I cared to admit. Still, if anyone could understand it would be Danny.

"I needed some time away from all this. I needed to get away," I tried to explain.

"I am here to protect you, Nadine. If I don't know where you are, I can't do my job. I was worried half out of my mind."

I hadn't thought about Danny worrying about me. I hadn't thought about anything except wanting to get away. The pressure was starting to get to me, and I had needed a release. I needed a tiny intermission from it all.

I would have been happy if someone had offered me with another reset on my life but this time I wouldn't want to remember. When my family and the Council sent me into the Real my soul had been merged with the vessel I had been provided. Because of that, I had in essence became Nadine Ruth. I was born into the body of a child who had been destined to die. My memories of my life before in the Realm were all but gone. That is, until I vanquished Lou triggering them to slowly returned. I had begun to remember but my swiss cheese brain could only remember old memories unless triggered by something else. That made being at home in the Realm frustrating for both me and the family. Still, I had the feeling the family would rather my memories never returned. I was only beginning to understand why, and I completely agreed with them.

I wanted to be back in blissful ignorance. Perhaps that's why all my memories had not returned to me already. Somewhere inside me I already knew I didn't want them back. I wanted to remain in the dark of who I once was. I feared finding out I was anything but the person I believed me to be. The whispers of stories I had gleamed over the past year had not been one of a happy complicit princess. I was a wild child, doing as she saw fit regardless of what others thought. I wasn't that person anymore but what I did to Danny showed I was very much capable of being that girl again. I wished I could reset and forget all about the damage I caused to my family in the Realm and to my friends in the Real. I most of all wished Danny wasn't so upset with me.

"I am so sorry, Danny," I cried fat wet tears streaming down my face.

All the fury left Danny when he saw my tears. He wrapped his arms around me bringing me to him. He held me in silence as I cried. Danny had been my rock on more than one occasion already. He hadn't blinked when the SLAGs sent him to the Real as my guardian. I was acting like a spoiled child and not a very good friend. When I sniffed back the last of my tears, he handed me a tissue from the desk behind us. He leaned against the desk and let out a long sigh.

"We are a team, Nadine. You have to keep me informed if you are going to deviate from the plan. I will always keep your confidence, but I need you to be honest with me at all times. You need to promise me you will do this," he lectured me.

"I will," I promised him.

He nodded and took a long moment before asking, "Why don't you tell me what actually happened with AJ now?"

I wasn't sure how to explain what happened. One minute we were joking around and then the next we were kissing. I made it clear that it wasn't just AJ kissing me. I had kissed him back. I had felt something too and that was why it had been even more important I had my day out with Carter. I didn't like feeling so out of control as I did with AJ. It was wild and unhinged. It had felt good, but it didn't feel like me, not completely anyway. It was like I had been tapping into some dormant part of me and that part didn't mesh well with the me I was now. There was something familiar about AJ though. It was like a piece of my past was opening up to me again but still too far away to hold on to. I felt like I was floating between what I knew and some hidden knowledge just beyond my reach. Being with Carter grounded me while AJ did anything but.

That was what I told Danny as I poured my heart out to him. He sat there for a long moment until his features held long shadows from the setting sun. My predicament was not an easy one. The friend in him wanted to help me. He just didn't know how. I didn't know how to help myself either. I was stuck between two worlds, both of which were equal to me in almost every way possible.

"I wouldn't wish what you have been going through on anyone, Nadine. Any of what you have gone through, none of it. I think, at least for now anyway, you should probably stay clear of making any major decisions with either guys though. You know all the reasons why. I don't have to recap them for you. I don't want to see anyone, especially you, getting hurt by any decisions made in haste. Once the Dark Lord has been dealt with then you will be in a better position to deal with destiny may have in store for you," Danny told me trying to be diplomatic.

He was right. I knew the reasons for and against each choice I could make. If I let myself get any closer to Carter and the tether was broken, I would be devastated at the loss of him and the Real. I was not capable of giving Carter up. I tried and had failed miserably. I could not engage in a relationship with AJ in the Realm though while with Carter. It felt too wrong. I needed to do as Danny suggested. I needed to bide my time and see what destiny had in store for me. I would stay the course and keep moving one baby step at a time. I still had no idea what I would do if I saw AJ again. I tried not to think about it. He was probably long gone anyway. I had tossed him pretty good after all. What guy would stick around after that?

Chapter 6

Carter

I found myself in Sam's basement punching the bag hard wondering where I had gone wrong with Nadine. I could feel her pulling further and further away from me. No matter what I did though I was helpless to stop it. Everything that had happened over the summer was a culmination of problems that had been seeping into our relationship for a while. Ever since Nadine's grandfather had passed away, she had been different. She was keeping secrets from me. The Nadine I knew and loved never in a million years kept anything from me. This Nadine though was not the same girl I had fallen in love with. She had actually admitted that she was keeping things from me but was unable to tell me what it was she was hiding.

I thought our day out had been the beginning of a new start for us. We had laughed and made out. I thought she was close to finally confiding in me all the things she had been hiding. The day had ended though with nothing being revealed. Then, the next day I found her with that interloper again. They had been talking in hushed tones when I approached the next morning and stopped speaking all together when I was close. I inquired about a possible night out to make up for not being able to spend the night with Nadine since she had to work. I was shocked when she completely blew me off. I got angry when she told me why.

Josh would be working at Mr. Fong's with her and she had to show him around the place before his first afternoon. Nadine was blowing me off for Coma Boy. That sent my cackles up really quick. Josh Groves had been a jock and followed a completely different circle before his accident. I wasn't even sure how he even met Nadine. I wished he had never met Nadine at all. He was causing a dent in the little time I had with her as it was. She had already doubled down her time at the studio. Adding Coma Boy into the mix just made it worse. The boy was a nuisance as it was and needed to go back to his own click.

 Sam sensed problems brewing inside me and stopped lifting weights. He sat up and looked at me as he said, "So whose head are we pretending that is or do I even have to ask?"

"I don't get it. All I want to do is spend time with my girl and I can't even do that anymore," I voiced my concerns knowing I would get an honest opinion from Sam.

"Have you talked to Nadine about all this," Sam inquired.

I sighed back my frustration before saying, "I tried to tell Nadine, but I can never get her alone more than a few minutes. Everywhere we go it seems Coma Boy shows up. I end up getting mad and then she ends up getting mad and then it goes downhill from there."

It was true after all. I knew I could be a bit of a hothead, but she was bringing it out in me. I couldn't handle the silence. Lie to me if you need to, but don't ignore me. I rather she not lie either but I would take what I could get at that point.

"Well, it can't help that you keep calling Josh Coma Boy," Sam stated.

"I know but he irks me," I conceded.

"I don't know what to tell you, Cartman. All I know is that girl has eyes only for you."

But did she really? I wasn't feeling the love. I wasn't feeling loved at all from Nadine and it wasn't just me. I knew I was not making this up all on my own. Others had to see it too.

"If that's true then why is it she spends so much time with Josh and not me? It just doesn't make any sense."

"We don't know for sure it is Josh taking up all her time," Sam argued. When I gave him a knowing look he then added, "How do you know? I mean really."

This was going to look bad, but I could be honest with Sam. "I saw them together on more than one occasion. He was there last night at Mr. Fong's waiting for her. She never invites me to watch her work anymore, but he was there."

"So, you are spying on her now?"

I had enough. I was beginning to feel like a peeping tom, and it wasn't a good feeling. I hated admitting I was following her around. At first, I tried to pass it off as just trying to be a protective boyfriend. I don't know what it was now, but my motives had definitely changed. All her secrets aside, I needed to know why she was spending so much time with Josh. What did he have that made him able to get passed all her walls? Nadine had been throwing up a lot of walls lately but not for Josh. He had an all access pass to her all the time. It hurt to watch yet I couldn't look away. I was losing her to Coma Boy. I could feel it deep down inside. That was why I took to stalking her.

"Damn it! That's the only way I get to see her is by stalking her!! Don't you see? Something is really wrong," I yelled before punching the bag hard.

Sam stood up and moved to me. He put a comforting hand on my shoulder and let me breath out my frustration. It felt good to let it out. After a couple minutes Sam asked, "What can we do to make it better?"

I shook my head. I didn't know what would make things better with me and Nadine. I had no clue where to go from there. I knew I still wanted to be with her, but I just didn't know how we could survive everything that had gone on between us. I didn't know how to move forward with her but knew I could definitely not be without her. I was open to advice.

"I think a gesture of support might work. You know, show her you are by her side no matter what. Show her you are the only man for her," Sam suggested.

I chuckled before saying, "And I thought I was the girly one between the two of us."

"Hey. All I am saying is you will have to put yourself out there to keep your girl. That's all. There ain't nothing girly about that," he said defended himself.

"Okay. Any suggestions then on how," I asked.

"Not a clue."

"You're a big help."

Sam winked at me before moving back to his weights. He smiled saying, "I try."

We continued with our workout, but my mind was not into it. I was trying to figure out just how to be a better boyfriend when my girlfriend was M.I.A. all the time. All I knew for sure was that something big was going on with Nadine and she didn't feel like she could tell me. That alone had me worried. There was never a time until now that Nadine felt she could not tell me something. Whatever it was, I was seriously worried for her. Jealousy aside. I was worried more now for Nadine than I was when she was still living at home with her mom and Bart.

My mind couldn't fathom what was going on. I couldn't imagine anything worse than the savage brutality she had suffered under Bart. He had abused her physically, but he had never gotten an opportunity to enact his sexual plans for her. She had run away, running straight for me. She had told me what happened or at least I thought she had told me everything that happened. She downed two bottles of Nyquil and ended up in the hospital the very next night. I had blamed myself just as much as Bart because I had rejected her after she rebuked my own horny teenager advances. I had been the epitome of a gentleman since then though. It didn't matter though. We had not been the same since. Nadine had spent the summer alone only to end up in the hospital because of a false pregnancy. False pregnancy when she told us all she was still a virgin. I confronted her again about the situation and she had actually broken up with me. We barely had just gotten back together two weeks when Coma Boy showed up on the scene. He had her ear and she had stopped confiding in me all together. All I ever wanted to do was love her, help her anyway I could. I couldn't help her if I didn't know the truth. I would never get to the truth if I couldn't get her alone. Maybe Sam was right though. My pressuring her wasn't helping whatever she was going through. I needed to be a better boyfriend. I had to figure out how to be there for her even while she was pushing me away.

Chapter 7

Nadine

It had been a week since I ran out on AJ. There was no sign of him in the Realm nor any sign of Lou in the Real. While the first irritated me, the latter had me more concerned. We still had no clue what vessel Lou was using. There had been brief mention about coma patients disappearing from various hospitals in the area, but the coverage had been so brief and provided no real information. Danny tried to use his group therapy session mandated by Josh's doctors as a way to gain more information, but the doctors refused to speak about it in his group. We were running into dead ends left and right. With every passing day, Lou was merging more with his vessel and it would be near impossible to pick him out of the masses soon. He could be sitting right next to us and we would be none the wiser. I feared when Lou finally made himself known the body count would be outrageous. Each day we went without word, I grew more and more worried. I looked at every strange face in the crowd of students and wondered if Lou was hiding amongst them. Everyone was the enemy until proven otherwise.

It wasn't until I walked into my English class that I knew something was amiss. I could feel something off, but I couldn't tell where it was coming from. Carter was already in his seat waiting for me to sit by him. Josh stole my glance the moment I walked in. He could feel it too but had also not been able to place the cause. Where was it coming from? There were several new faces since the new year had begun. It could be any of them. One of them had to be possessed. One of them may very well be Lou.

Someone in the room was definitely not the person they claimed to be. Someone was a traveler just like Danny and just like me.

"Good morning, Ladies and Gentlemen. Please let me introduce myself. My name is Mr. Xavier Jacobs and I will be filling in for Mrs. Brookstone for the foreseeable future," the man in front of the class announced with a kind smile.

His smile was kind but there was something not quite kind about it at the same time. I shook it off and looked back at Josh as I took my seat. He shook his head as if to tell me he couldn't identify where the bad vibes were coming from. I had to stop my search though because Carter was looking at me very irked since I had yet to address him. His gaze kept drifting between Josh and me as if he was trying to catch us. Catch us doing what I was unsure. I knew our silent communication had not gone unnoticed though and wanted to kick myself. Still, there was a threat in the room to Carter and every other human in there. I tried to look passed Carter's uncertain ego and find the cause. We spent the better part of the class trying to find the source to no avail. Whoever it was had blended with its host vessel enough I was unable to read them properly.

When class ended, we filed out with the new teacher wishing us a good day. All class long the way Mr. Jacobs spoke had me cringing. He seemed too eager to be liked by the students. I felt bad for the man. He was trying way too hard. I knew what it was like to be new, so I felt sorry for him. I had been new to a world I couldn't recall not so long ago. It was painful watching him and I wished I could be of more help to him. I didn't have much time to dwell on him though. I had a murdering maniac to find.

Carter kissed me quickly rushing to his next class. It was on the other end of the school and he would have to haul ass to get there in time. He didn't want to leave me, but he couldn't cut class again. Not unless he wanted his folks to find out. I had more important things to worry about anyway. I waited for Danny, who came barreling out the door moments later.

"I wrote down some potentials but couldn't get a clear reading on any of them," Danny said handing me the list.

I nodded, looking at the list. There were a few I knew we could cross off right away. They were individuals who were odd birds, but I had known for a long time. That meant they were not recently possessed. Only someone who had been in a coma could be possessed. The names of those who were known entities were crossed off immediately. That meant we had four unsure since I didn't recognize the names. These were people I had never met before that school year. That also meant they could have been in the vessels for a while. It made sense since we didn't recognize them as possessed right away. That also meant Danny and I had a lot of work to do. We would have some recon ahead of us to determine if any of them were who we were looking for.

"Hurry along, children. The world waits for no one," our new teacher said happily.

I hadn't even heard him sneak up behind us. I shivered at the amount of glee he was giving off. We headed to our next classes making plans to meet up later to scope out the first name on the list. I couldn't help but feel as if eyes were burning cold at me. when I turned around all I saw was Mr. Jacobs in the hallway smiling. His smile was meant to be pleasant, but I couldn't help but think it was anything but. Shivering, I hurried inside my next class. Anything to be away from that stare.

Soubackalou

She was here. I had found her.

It took all of me not to snatch her up and do horrible, deviant things to her right there in those halls of education. My vessel craved the idea. I had to steady myself though. This was not a sprint I had been planning for but a marathon. The end game would be the carving of flesh from bone. First though, we had to play with our food. While physical pain was all well and good, I relished more. To truly torture someone on a psychological level, that made the meat taste so better when devoured. Her flesh would be begging to be destroyed by the time I was done with her and I would give her such a final release that the bards would write about for centuries. We would be legends in both worlds at the horrors I would do to my feisty little princess. After all, I owed her a lingering death for taking my throne from me and then having the audacity to vanquish me. She deserved everything I had planned for her and more. It was a shame I could only kill her once.

First though, I would have to dispatch all the fleshy obstacles in my way. The princess has company. There had been more than just us two travelers in that tiny school room. I could sense the interloper and surmised they could sense me as well. By the time class ended and I had educated those little monsters, I had it narrowed down to two individuals who may be travelers. I would browse through their academic records later to see if either may be the one I was looking for. It was good being an educator of the masses. It gave one access to all types of useful information. That would come in handy for enacting my plans.

"Oh, my sweet little princess. You may have infinite power in the Realm but here you are so very vulnerable. Here you will succumb in such definite agony. It will be glorious," I whispered to myself.

I watched her moving down the hallway. She stopped looking back at me. I knew she could feel my gaze. She didn't suspect me yet though. If she had she would have most likely confronted me already. She was positively clueless, and I was the apex predator circling my unsuspecting prey. When she looked back, I pretended to be ushering in a new batch of monsters to educate.

"Who are you," asked one of the more snobbish new students entering my territory.

"I am Mr. Jacobs. I will be providing you your education today," I informed the little snob.

She scoffed at me heading into class tapping away on her phone. I had to tamper down the urge again. The young ignorant thing was lucky I had a role to play. Had I been free as I was in the Realm, the girl would have not made it into the room and her flesh would be my winter coat as a reminder of who I truly was. I wasn't the Dark Lord Soubackalou in the Real though. I was almost as insignificant as she was. I was merely a facilitator of education but I planned to educate them all very soon. My vessel's needs would be sated soon enough.

Nadine

The day was a bust. No new leads and I had to admit I was more than a bit frustrated. The silver lining around Danny's eyes had begun to fade. Lou had a head start when it came to how long he had been in the Real. Without the tell-tale sign from the eyes, I was unsure how we would be able to identify the offenders. Danny, though just as worried as me about it, had a mission. Someone in that classroom today was exhibiting signs of being from another world. We had list to work with. That was enough for Danny. I was not so easily appeased though. I was becoming anxious and it was starting to show. At least, with the people who cared about me anyway. That and the ever so inquisitive Miss Pauline.

I had to let Danny head off on his own to hunt for Lou. I had a session to attend with Miss Pauline. She was waiting for me browsing over college brochures I was sure was for students who actually had a future in the Real. It wasn't that I was not smart enough for college. College was a far fetching dream for me. I was a princess from another world, not just a junior in high school. My life was already planned out for me. Well, one of my lives anyway. My days were numbered in the Real. It could be tomorrow or a year from now, but my family would find a way to break my tether. When that happened, I would have no choice but to give up the Real.

It was those somber thoughts rolling around in my head when I entered her office. She noticed my sour mood even before I opened my mouth. She didn't remark about it at first though. Instead, she jotted down some notes while she asked me about my week. I pretended to be bored by the question trying to brush it off. After all, my week had been about searching for my nemesis. I couldn't tell her that though.

"How has Mr. Groves been handling his transition back into society," Miss Pauline asked me suddenly.

That took me by surprise. I had been assigned to Josh by his request. Miss Pauline was seeing him as regularly as she was seeing me. Her asking me about how I felt his transition was doing, that sent up red flags all over the place. I had to proceed with caution. I knew she would never guess our true relationship, but I needed to ensure the wayward guidance counselor didn't get too suspicious about Josh. I needed him, at least until Lou was sent packing.

"Fine, I guess. We only have a couple of classes together, so I don't see him that often," I lied.

"From what I hear you have more than a couple classes with Mr. Groves. I have seen you taking your lunchbreak with him often enough. You are also working at the same employer."

"Have you been spying on us," I asked her concerned.

"I am responsible for the health and mental wellbeing of all my students, Miss Ruth. I like to keep a closer eye on those who need it," she told me plainly.

I narrowed my eyes trying to gage her. Had she had been watching Josh or me? I knew Miss Pauline was not Lou. She had been our guidance counselor for the last two years. No, not Lou. That didn't mean she didn't have a dark side. She may have been touched by Lou's evil in one way or another. I was no longer sure if I could trust her or not.

"Correct me if I am wrong but this hour is supposed to be about me. If you want to know about Josh, ask him yourself."

"Your friendship with Mr. Groves may be healthy for him having recently come out of his coma. He has yet to embrace is old life though. Also, I am seeing strife between you and your own friends. Perhaps it is because of this new relationship. I wanted to see what your thoughts were. I didn't mean to offend. I am just here to help, Nadine," she told me calmly. She was raking my nerves at how calm she always was.

"Well I didn't know keeping up on high school gossip was part of your job. Josh and I are friends. Period, the end. If you want dirt on him, I suggest you find someone else to probe," I countered.

I was a bit harsh with her, but she hit a nerve. If she was looking closer at Josh, we had need to worry. If she was watching me, I wasn't sure what that meant. Two stints in the hospital, one under her watch. I could see where she would be more prone to following me closer. Either way though, we needed to be more careful. I would warn Danny when we got back to the Realm to watch his words with Miss Pauline more cautiously. They might be kindred spirits as educators, but she was not someone to embrace. We had to be more careful about what the Real saw of our relationship. Miss Pauline was only part of that problem. I didn't want to reflect on the other relationship my friendship with Josh Groves was causing difficulties for. We didn't have time for games though. Lou was close by and I knew he would strike sooner to later. We had to be ready, no matter who it put off.

Chapter 8

Nadine

Things seemed to get back to a semblance of normal in the Realm. I continued on with my lessons with Danny and Riley. I had begun to grasp a better handle on my powers. I could pull a fireball at will with no issue. Riley was attempting to teach me higher leveled magic, but he was coming away more frustrated than anything else. In order for him to show me any tricks, it took him some time to gather the amount of energy needed. I, on the other hand, only needed to will it and the power was mine. After an hour or so, Riley would end up sending me to Vega because he could not expel the amount of energy needed to continue my training. Vega graduated me to more sword work with Quintus. I wasn't sure if I was ready, and Quintus was not one to take it easy on me. I found that out first and foremost. I came out of sparring with him feeling my muscles burning. It felt good compared to the frustrating days in the Real.

Our search for Lou was still not bearing any fruit. We checked the background on every suspect Danny had on his list to no avail. I was beginning to wonder if I had truly felt another from the Realm nearby or was it because I expected to and reacted accordingly. Lou was in the Real. We knew that for a fact. He had not made himself known to us yet though. It gave me chills thinking about what he was out there and what he possibly was doing. He was capable of monstrous things, as I witnessed to firsthand. The Real was not ready for the likes of the Dark Lord.

I thought that perhaps Riley would be able to give us a clue into Lou or his whereabouts. I asked one day while training for his possible assistance. Riley consulted a scrying bowl filled with essence from the Power Crystal. It was how he was able to gleam future possibilities, as did his previous predecessors had many times before. Riley sat there in a deep concentration for a long while. I was beginning to get impatient when suddenly he gasped stepping back from the bowl.

"What is it," I asked.

"I see a rift coming. I see very hard times ahead for our people," he told me, still staring at the bowl.

"A rift? What kind of a rift?"

Riley strained balling his fists against the table as he said, "I don't know. There is such power – It is hard to tell."

The future was like branches on a tree. Each one held its own possible path. Asking Riley to divine a particular path was like swimming in turbulent waters. Only the very trained could maneuver through such waves and even then, they would not be without issues. Still, we had to press the matter. If it was part of my future he saw, I needed to know if Lou was entangled in anyway. I needed to know if the Real was at risk.

"Is it Lou?" Please say no.

"No. That I can say with much certainty. It is definitely not the Dark Lord." Riley looked from the bowl to the Crystal. "Only someone who can harness the power will be able to cause this rift."

"But if it is not Lou then who," I asked confused.

"I don't know but the Dark Lord is part demon. No demon can harness the power of the Crystal. It would kill him without question." Riley shivered uncontrollably. "I do not see Soubackalou in this vision at all."

I shivered thinking about the possibilities as I asked, "What do you see?"

He seemed to choose his words before he told me, "I see Detoriola and all the other kingdoms in ruins. I see the Power Crystal gone from its chamber. I see death."

I sat back shocked. If demons could not touch the Crystal, then how can it be gone from the chamber? What could cause so much death and destruction Riley had foreseen? I couldn't even think of anything worse than Lou. Perhaps the infamous Lord Evil I kept hearing about? I wasn't even sure if he was a demon or not. Most suspected he was at least part demon. Lord Evil was said to be the powerfullest evil being in the entire Realm. He could be like Lou and have human DNA coursing through him. Was this the power he saw in his vision? Still, even humans had a hard time touching the Crystal. Riley had to use special gloves to work the magic from the Crystal's leavenings. What could cause such a rift and take the Crystal from its chamber?

"That is impossible. No one can remove the Crystal from this chamber," I said doubting his words.

"I cannot deny what I see. I cannot deny seeing you there as well."

"You saw me in this vision?"

Riley closed his eyes and recalled, "I saw you emerging from the ashes left of the fallen. There were others with you, but I see you the strongest. This rift will change us all, princess. Even you."

"What does that mean? Change me how?"

The Guardian did not answer. I watched him stare at the Crystal as if searching for something. The vision was incomplete but one thing for certain, I was in his vision. That had me very nervous. Whatever was going to happen I would be front and center for. I would be involved somehow with the apocalypse he saw. Whatever happened would change me somehow. He never said for good or bad. There was a prophecy that followed that logic just the same. Neither had said if it was for a force of good or evil. What the hell was going to happen to my people? More importantly what was going to happen to me?

I found myself thinking these very thoughts as I was heading to my lesson with Quintus. It was then I happened to spot AJ heading toward the training fields. He had a staff slung across his back. No doubt he was heading to get some training in. It shocked me seeing him again to the point I stopped in my tracks. I had not laid eyes on him since I tossed him magically weeks ago. He hadn't seen me yet. I could have let him go on his way none the wiser. The pull inside me he caused when I was near was not liking that idea though. I found myself calling out to him instead.

AJ looked up and also stopped in his tracks when he saw me. His momentary surprise changed. AJ looked angry. He shook his head and turned around, heading back the way he came. I couldn't help myself. I pursued him. It wasn't until we were both at the entrance of the Conduit doorway to his Dreamscape that I caught up with him. I grabbed his arm, stopping him from entering.

"What," he barked, pulling away.

"I am sorry, AJ," I said to him.

"Really? What for exactly because I know why I am mad? Do you," he barked again.

Man, but he was pissed. I really wasn't sure why. Sure, I had tossed him like a rag doll with my powers, but he hadn't seemed upset by that at the time. He had actually seemed turned on by it if I remembered correctly. I did run away though. I hadn't sought him out afterwards either. Still, he hadn't actually sought me out either. I had no idea what his problem was. I just knew he was angry with me.

I shrugged my shoulders trying to put words together.

"You really don't get it, do you? I am not the kind of person your family wants you hanging out with, Nadine. Its best you let bygones be bygones and forget I even existed."

"Did someone say something to you? I don't get where all this is coming from," I asked confused by what he was saying to me.

"No. No one had to say anything to me. I can read between the lines. You are a princess. I am nobody going nowhere. You are a traveler of worlds. I only get to see glimpses of other lands through the Dreamscape. You are beautiful inside and out. I am a black spot on existence. It's okay. I get it.

Why don't you go run back to your family and your boyfriend in the Real. I don't need your pity," he told me.

AJ was trying to hurt me. He was trying to push me away. The more he spoke though the more I knew he needed me. He needed me in his life, and I needed to be there for him. I understood exactly how he was feeling because I had felt those exact feelings every day of my life. He thought he was the black sheep in his family as did I. I was born from a forbidden relationship and had been a black mark on our family ever since. AJ thought he wasn't good enough for his family and I lived with that feeling every day as well. I knew him because I was him. We were kindred spirits. Perhaps that is why I was so drawn to him. We were cut from the same cloth.

"AJ, you aren't going to make me stop being your friend by saying mean things about yourself. I know you better than that," I told him.

He scoffed. "You don't know me."

"Black sheep of the family. Misunderstood. Only looking to be like everyone else. I know you, AJ, because I am you. We are the same," I explained putting my hand on his shoulder.

He looked at me trying hard to stay angry. His anger was his shield. It was what he used to fend off affection from the people he cared about the most. If he couldn't stay angry with me, he wouldn't have anything to defend himself. I was getting to him and I knew it. That was why he was trying to push me away, but I wouldn't let him.

"I just want to be your friend," I told him sincerely.

"My friend? You want to be just friends with me," he asked moving closer to me.

I could feel the heat rising between us. This hadn't been a good idea. I should have let him go on his way. I was not in control of myself around AJ as it was. I had no idea why I would even suggest being friends with AJ. Every time he came close to me my body reacted to him in a very excited and too friendly way. It betrayed me, my body. I was a slave to this pull we had together and there was nothing I could do about it.

"There is so much going on in my life right now, AJ. I can't offer you any more than that. Please, respect that," I begged him, taking a step back.

AJ matched my steps. His hand ran down my arm as a crooked smile graced his lips. "I think you have a lot to offer me. You just need the right motivation."

AJ's mouth claimed mine. My mouth was saying no but my body was screaming yes. The damn betraying body of mine. His arm wrapped around my waist pulling me closer to him. I didn't resist. I couldn't, I was under his spell. Damn it all to hell but I needed AJ's touch like I was a dying man in the desert needing water. Consequences of what this meant in the Real were the least of my concerns. Everything seemed to melt away. Had he asked me to give himself to him in that moment, I was not sure I could have said no to him. I was enthralled by him. I needed some divine assistance if I was going to stop. As luck would have it, assistance came in the form of something a bit more demonic in nature.

"OH, dear. That doesn't look like your boyfriend, Miss Ruth. You should be ashamed of yourself," a chilling and familiar voice came interrupting us.

We both turned to find Lou standing there, looking smug at us both. AJ immediately pulled me behind him, drawing his staff. That just made Lou chuckle, amused. I sidestepped AJ, standing next to him. We were both ready to take on the foul halfling.

"Back off, Lou. This is no business of yours," I growled, gathering a fireball in my hand.

"I beg to differ, princess. That is my nephew you are leading on after all," Lou said calmly.

"Nephew," I repeated confused. The fireball I had been concentrating on diminished. I looked between Lou and AJ shocked. Lou was AJ's uncle? How the hell was that possible? I didn't get the chanced to inquire further though.

"Be gone, you heinous filthy beast," AJ yelled, angrily.

 AJ lashed out with his staff. Lou drew his sword, seeing a fight was inevitable. They clashed several times, staff meeting sword. Lou was calm and collected but also eager for the battle. AJ was swinging angrily and became erratic with each counterblow dealt. AJ was losing his control and fast. I saw the inevitable and didn't want him to get hurt. As it was, it looked like Lou was just there to taunt AJ and not really hurt him anyway. Lou was not showing the telltale signs of when he loses control of his facilities. I knew those signs as I had caused then enough. I shot a quick fireball at Lou. Not big enough to damage him but enough to draw his attention for the moment. Gripping AJ from behind, I pulled him back to me as I hurdled another fireball at Lou. He deflected both easily but took several steps back as a precaution. He knew I could vanquish if I really put my mind to it, so he was not taking any chances. He continued to back up looking victorious in his retreat.

"Another time then. See you in school, princess," Lou waved, before disappearing through a nearby Conduit doorway. He had done what he came to do. That was enough now for him.

Once Lou was out of sight, I turned to AJ who was pacing angrily. AJ was Lou's nephew. How did I not know this? The others had failed to mention it to me, and I suspected that was on purpose. AJ had a dark side and I now knew where it came from. Was that the reason I was so attracted to him? I had so many questions, but AJ did not look in any shape to answer them.

"You see why we can't be friends. How can we be friends when that halfling has rotted our family tree? How could you even want to be near someone like that," AJ bellowed before taking off as well.

I stood there looking in the direction of where he disappeared to. He was right and yet so wrong. AJ was family to the beast who had raped me. If I was smart, I would run away and not look back. Still, it begged the question, did the rest of my family know about his family history. Unicorn had married AJ's brother after all. That made Antonio kin to Lou as well. They had tried to scare me off of AJ, not solely because of his pedigree but because of his wild spirit. Did they really think AJ's dark side was all there was to him? AJ may have been kin to Lou, but he was nothing like the demon halfling. There was something more about him that drew me to him. He was a lost soul begging to be found. The question really was would I let him flee from the light or let him be consumed by his own inner demons?

I could stand there and let him disappear again. I could pretend there was nothing happening between us and move on with my life. It's what the family wanted. It's what he said he wanted. It would be for the best, especially since I was in love with Carter. AJ was not good for my relationship with Carter or my family. I should just let him disappear. It was what was best for everyone involved. When did I ever do what's best for me though?

Chapter 9

I didn't seek AJ out right away after his revelation. Instead, I found Danny. He was in the library, reading a scroll on the finer arts of SLAG negotiations when I located him. Danny was concentrating on finding a solution for Lou in the Real. It was what I should have been concentrating on as well, but I had been distracted by my life. I had been distracted by AJ again. Danny looked up surprised, but his face changed as soon as he saw mine.

"What's wrong," he asked concerned as he stood up.

I sunk into a leather padded chair with a long sigh before saying, "So much. So much and I need to talk to someone about it."

"Well then, it's ideal that I am a good listener then. What happened," He said sitting beside me.

I told him about my encounter with AJ and how Lou showed up revealing his relationship to AJ. The revelation did not seem to surprise Danny as I thought it would. I guess that shouldn't have surprised me either though. Danny knew a hell of a lot more than he let on at times. That revelation was no different.

"Does it bother you that he is a relation to the Dark Lord," Danny asked when I was done.

"What? No. I could care less about that. We can't choose our family. I am damn sure evidence of that. I just don't understand why he reacted the way he did."

Danny nodded in understanding before saying, "Soubackalou's birth has always been a point of pain for his family. You see, his mother was a succubus that seduced Soubackalou's father. The father had been a kind and decent man from good stock. Not royalty like yourself but closer than most. He had two fully human children given to him by his wife when he had succumbed to the wiles of the beast. The Dark Lord has always a blight on the family because of what his mother was. It is that connection driving Antonio so hard at being a force for good."

"What about AJ? Why does everyone think he is so bad," I asked.

"While Antonio chose to follow the steadfast path of his father, AJ choose to follow in the footsteps of his mother who was a gypsy. Her gypsy blood is strong in AJ and he has always embraced the lifestyle with open arms. The gypsies cannot be governed by any kingdom nor the Council. Not unless they commit a major crime against humanity anyway. Because of this, they are feared and in turn hated by many."

AJ's gypsy nature was strong in him. I could tell from the stories he told me. His lifestyle had always been a wanderer by nature. He was the exact opposite of his big brother. Antonio thrust himself into being the best warrior possible, settling for 2nd only to my sister, his own wife. Free spirit had always been a blight to my family. It appeared ours was not the only one who thought this way though. The free spirit of the gypsies was condemned, looked down upon by those they thought their betters, my family included. It wasn't right. After all, the Realm had many types of creeds and races amongst its people. Each type of being was accepted without judgement. The gypsies should be no different. They loved just the same as any other race.

"But their father fell in love with the mother. They couldn't be all bad if that happened."

"True but unfortunately AJ's mother left home soon after he was born. Life with her husband had become too mundane for someone so wild. She craved the gypsy freedom she once had. It was several years later AJ went in search of her in hopes to bring her home. I don't suppose he found her, but he did find something else he liked in the lifestyle. After some time, AJ gave up his search but refused to come home. He had found a new one with the gypsies. It was because of this he has been labeled a bad seed."

I thought about what Danny had said. His description of the gypsies and their way of life seemed familiar. I could picture it in my head so clearly. I wasn't sure if it was because I was remembering them first-hand or because it was something I craved as well. I craved freedom from the crown. I wanted a life of my own, not one so viewed under the microscopic perspectives of the Council or my family. The appeal was alluring to say the least. I wasn't hundred percent sure it was just the lifestyle drawing me in though or AJ himself. His fury when he took on Lou had sent chills of excitement down my spine. His passion was so overwhelming.

"What do you plan to do with this new information," Danny asked curiously.

"I am not sure. What I do know is AJ needs someone in his corner. He needs a friend and I want to be that for him."

"Just a friend," Danny asked curiously.

I looked at Danny but couldn't answer the question. I had told Danny about the kiss AJ and I had shared. He knew there was something brewing between us but thankfully did not comment. I wasn't sure of the answer myself. All I knew is AJ was meant to be in my life. The rest I would sort out later.

I decided to let the situation with AJ lie for the rest of the evening. There was not much I could do about it since AJ had run off anyway. I had a full day of school to think about and the hunt for Lou's vessel to continue. With no more suspects in mind, I wasn't sure how to proceed though. Lou had made himself known again in the Realm though. He had been pushed back pretty quick by me and AJ. I feared he would rear his not so ugly head with a vengeance in the Real. Lou wasn't one for fighting on a leveled playing field.

My head was wrapped around trying to find another way to find Lou when I nearly bumped right into Mr. Jacobs, who was standing in the doorway. I caught myself quickly though but dropped several papers I had been holding. Mr. Jacobs bent down helping me pick up my papers. Our fingers brushed accidentally causing me to cringe away. His touch felt oily like I had been touched by a swamp. It felt wrong. I gathered the papers to me taking a step back away from him. I wanted to put some distance between us.

He was a squirrely older man. His form was fit but not overly muscled. I could tell he had recently begun working out though. If I didn't find his presence disturbing, I would probably have enjoyed his features. His dark locks were slicked back away from his face making his rounded glasses seem even bigger on his face than they already were. Despite his distorted but fairly average features being near him set my teeth on end. I wasn't sure why, but I didn't want to be anywhere near the man.

"Good Morning, Miss Ruth. It's a pleasure to see you this morning," He said with a huge grin.

To any ordinary person, the man would come across as an ordinary teacher, happy to be there. I had a sneaky suspicion though he was much more than that. I couldn't say why exactly, maybe it was how I felt when he touched me. I had no real evidence, but I was sure I had found the vessel we were looking for. Even without the silver around the eyes, I knew that this man was what we had been looking for. At the very least, the new teacher was not who he said he was. I had to tell Danny. He would be able to tell for sure. I rushed past Mr. Jacobs hurrying in search of Danny.

"Have a good day, Miss Ruth," Mr. Jacobs called after me waving a paper in his hand.

I cringed heading away from him. I needed to get away from him as fast as I could. Not so surprisingly, I found Josh in the library. I mused at the fact Danny couldn't keep away from a room full of books and knowledge. He was enthralled by whatever he was reading to the point he didn't even hear me approach or acknowledge me until I sat down next to him. He looked up shocked to see me there. Second time in less than 24 hours I caught Danny by surprise.

"Hey. I hadn't planned to see you again until next period. Is everything okay," He asked concerned.

I launched into my encounter with Mr. Jacobs. He agreed that my concerns held enough weight to at least investigate the man. Josh stood up and moved into the computer room. He had taken quickly to electronic devices like the school computers. He was a fast learner though so it shouldn't surprise me. The Realm did not have anything like computers though. Danny punched in what he was looking for using the internet. He liked the internet since it helped in finding certain things quickly. In our world, it took weeks to go through the scrolls needed to research any subject. Danny marveled at the speed and amount of information was just at his fingertips. Still, I found him more often than not with a book in hand. Some things never changed.

"I found something. It does look like there was a Xavier Jacobs who recently recovered from injuries received after a car accident several years ago. There isn't much more on this site about it, but this may be fruitful," Josh said staring at other the articles scrolling down the screen.

"How should we proceed," I asked moving into unfamiliar territory.

"Let me continue to do some research. Let's see what else I can dig up," he said gleefully.

I had a feeling I could leave Danny there all day and he wouldn't notice I was gone. The guy lived for research. While he did his thing, I decided a little recon would be helpful. It wasn't like I could get into his personnel file or anything, but I could get a hold of his class schedule. I knew where he was twice a day all ready, my English and Creative Writing classes. I could track his other movements with little problem. Well, except while I was tracking Mr. Jacobs, I would be stealing more time from Carter. So yeah, problem. I knew once I established the schedule though Josh and I could split our time keeping eyes on him. This was slightly more important than one guy's feelings. Even if it was Carter. He would just have to understand. He couldn't understand though because I was still hiding the truth from him, a truth I could never tell him.

As I emerged from the computer room, I found Carter staring at me. I looked back quickly to see Josh still glued to the screen. I then looked to Carter again. He didn't say a word to me. He just balled his fists trying to hold in his anger. Panic shot through me sending up waves of panic. At the same time some papers on the nearby desk seemed to have been picked up by a breeze. I hadn't felt the breeze, but it was enough to move the papers.

"Carter, we were just doing some research," I told him defensively.

Carter hauled off and punched the nearby wall, plaster splintering around his fist. He then walked out of the library without a single word. That was not good. That was not good at all. I had plenty of reasons for Carter to be mad at me, but Josh was not one of them. How could I make him see that when life was forcing me to choose between him and what was right all the time? I was beginning to think doing the right thing was not the best option anymore. I should have hurried after him. I should have told him the truth and let the chips fall where they might. Instead though, I did the right thing yet again. The greater good prevailed. I went to find Mr. Jacobs.

I stood across the hall from Mr. Jacobs and the class he was about to teach. I watched him; my notebook held tightly against my chest. It felt odd spying, especially on a teacher. If it was Lou though, we had to know. I was at odds if I wanted it to be him or not. The last time I saw him he was engaged battling AJ, his own flesh and blood. It was so quick I didn't have a lot of time to process what was happening. Not like I did when he engaged us in battle. I had been filled with such rage because of what he had done to me. Lou had used my newborn child to be reborn. The child I had from the rape and torture I had endured by him. If this was Lou, I wasn't sure how to act. I didn't know if I was strong enough to defeat him there in the Real. As much anger and resentment, I had for Lou, I wasn't sure I could hurt the vessel he was wearing. The person he was wearing was innocent as far as I knew. As much as I despised Lou, Xavier Jacobs was just a means to an end for the Dark Lord.

Mr. Jacobs looked up as if he had sensed my presence. He looked at me with a bright smile. I narrowed my eyes at him. That only seemed to make him even more happy. I was about to cross the hall and confront him, damning the consequences when Carter moved in front of me suddenly. I looked up at him surprised.

"You weren't even going to see if I was okay, were you," he asked disgusted.

I looked at his hand. It was wrapped in an ace bandage. Served him right, hitting a wall like that for no reason. The knucklehead had hurt himself for no reason. Still, he was right. I hadn't tried to find him. I was consumed with finding Lou instead. My worlds were colliding, and Carter was suffering for it.

"You don't seem any worse for wear," I told him, trying to sound calm when I felt anything but that.

"Would you have even cared if I did more than sprain my hand?"

I should have been concerned. If everything had been right in the world, I would have been concerned. I would have been right beside him, nursing his wound for him. To be completely honest, he wouldn't have even gotten injured in the first place if not for me. Had my double life not been a thing, there would be no conflict between Carter and me. I would not be standing there stalking the new teacher. Instead, I would have probably been making out in the stacks in the library with Carter. My world was far from perfect though and I was tired of having to justify my every action all the time.

I sighed looking at him, "I am so tired of this, Carter. I have done nothing on the face of this earth to make you suspect me of anything. I wish you would stop acting like I have."

I hadn't lied. I had done nothing in that world, the Real. I couldn't necessarily say that of the Realm though. Still, Carter knew nothing of AJ. His fears were based on my friendship with Josh. In that sense, I had done nothing wrong. Josh was my friend and I was helping him through his re-introduction to society. There were much more heinous things to be worried about. Carter had no idea about what was lurking beneath the surface.

"Every time I find you, he is not far behind. When do I get my time alone with you? When will it be our time," he asked moving closer to me.

I cupped my hand against his cheek lightly. I had no idea what to tell him. All he wanted to do was be with me and I couldn't give him one thing he wanted. There was so much more important going on than our problems.

I wanted so much for the problems I was facing to just disappear. I wanted nothing more than to just be with Carter, the Realm be damned. That was not how my life worked though. There were bigger things at stake than the lovelorn.

"Are you okay, Nadine," a voice from behind us came.

"Like I said, never far behind," Carter said through clenched teeth.

I brought my other hand to his face stopping him from turning to Josh. I made him look into my eyes. I wanted him to not just see but feel what I had to say. I wanted him to feel it inside him and really believe me. "You have nothing to worry about. I am yours."

We stared at each other for a long moment before Carter looked away nodding. I kissed him lightly on the lips. He held me close before telling me he would see me later. I watched him head down the hall trying not to turn and knock Josh out. He would try anyway. Danny was getting better each day from his lessons with Vega. It would be a good fight either way. I knew if I didn't spend time with Carter soon, he and Josh would come to blows and I would not be able to do anything to stop it.

"You two better get to class. You wouldn't want to get in trouble," Mr. Jacobs sang the last part.

The bastard was enjoying the misery he was causing. I took a step forward ready to confront him again, but Danny grabbed my arm. He pulled me down the hall and away from Mr. Jacob. Good thing too because the anger inside me was starting to boil over. I could feel something building inside me. My hands were shaking. We had barely made it outside before I felt the power shoot from me. A blue streak of energy flew from my hands striking out. It was like lightning hitting a nearby tree. A big crack formed down the middle splitting it in two. Both Danny and I looked to the broken tree in shock.

"Did you -" Danny began but couldn't finish.

It was ridiculous. It couldn't be true. It had to be though. There was no other explanation for it. Somehow, some way, my powers had manifested in the Real. My fight with Bart, the breeze that was not a breeze in the library. Now the tree. It was true. My powers had followed me into the Real. I couldn't handle the ramifications of this new discovery. Not just yet anyway.

"Please don't tell the others, Danny," I begged unable to look away from the damaged tree.

He stood there looking at me shocked and unable to form a complete sentence. That was not good. It was not good at all. I had my powers in the Real. It was the last thing my family needed to hear. It was one more thing that made me different from everyone I knew. That wasn't the biggest issue though. If anyone knew my powers were active in the Real, it could be used against us. It could be used to justify Lou's stay. I couldn't have that. I needed to get him out of the Real and fast. Most of all, I didn't need anyone else finding out I was more of a freak than they originally thought.

Chapter 10

Soubackalou

It was naughty of me, I know. My vessel had been craving to touch her though. I had yearned to have her in my grasp again and the vessel knew it. It wanted to know first-hand what she felt like under its touch. My vessel wanted to feel her skin as I painted it red with her own blood. Just one touch would do for now though. When she dropped her papers, it gave me ample opportunity to do just that. I may have given the game away, but she would have figure out who I was eventually. She was smarter than she appeared. She had made that very apparent when I caught her spying on me at the end of the day. At least my reveal would be on my own terms though.

There had been an interesting turn of events I had spied. There seemed to be some friction with the pretty princess and her merry band of followers. Her indiscretions with my nephew and now this new development. I would have to mull over how these things could play into the grander scheme of things. Jealousy was a powerful tool and the princess was providing me ample opportunity to use it against her. I still needed to remain impartial though until I made my big reveal. She had been in such a rush to get away from me. I knew she had felt the evil my vessel contained. That in itself had been worth it. Still, both my vessel and I needed to satisfy our urges and soon. Otherwise I would get sloppy and we couldn't let that happen. After all, we were playing the long game. I couldn't let myself get caught blood red handed before the game was over. I needed an outlet and Mrs. Brookstone was beginning to bore me.

I looked out as the masses of meat tapping my pencil against my lips. "So many choices. How does one choose with such a lovely buffet?"

Last of the Dream Warriors – Jealousy

It was then a fellow educator found his way by my side. Arnie Anderson, math teacher. The bag of flesh had introduced himself to me on my very first day in the institution. He had been overly eager to befriend me. I could tell he was desperate for companionship. Typically, the type of soul I had used many times before and broken for giggles. He had been useful in finding out more about how the systems worked though. For that alone, he was still alive, but his usefulness was fading. I found him annoying at best.

"Hey Xavier. Ready for the weekend," Arnie asked with his very nasally voice.

I watched him adjust his glasses over his fat cheeks. He was not thin nor was he overly obese. He was hovering a fine line in between though. His thick thighs made music with the linen suit he wore every day. He always seemed to be sweating like a roasted pig. That did give me some ideas of how to sate my needs as well as be done with this constant pest. I could make more than a meal or two out of the lumpy specimen.

"Not much, Arnie. Perhaps you would want to come 'round for a bit of barbeque," I offered with a smile.

He eagerly accepted. The man had no life outside the walls of the school. He happily agreed to a meal. Little did he know the only barbeque I planned to have on menu would be those thick thighs. He happily wrote down my address before heading off to teach his class joyful about our little planned gathering. Now that I had a plan for satisfying the urges my vessel and I shared, I could teach my little monsters happily. I planned on a light lunch today because by nightfall my belly would be filled with something much more attractive than lukewarm mac and cheese from the school cafeteria.

I hurried home that evening to prepare. I had already disposed of the remains of a vagrant I had picked up shopping one evening as well as that of the unsuspecting girl scout who didn't realized more than cookies were needed to sate my tastes until it was too late. The vibrant Mrs. Brookstone had been holding up nicely, so I decided to keep her around a bit longer. Physically anyway. Her mental state was suspect at that point though. She had watched me as I carved up the little pigtailed beauty before having my way with my masterpiece. I had taken my time in savoring the little creature until I broke my new little pet. The little ones are so much more fragile but gave so many more thrills and screams. I would have to do something with Mrs. Brookstone though, at least until Arnie figured out what his fate would be.

I made sure she was gagged and tied up tightly before I showered and set the scene. The barbeque was fired up and ready to go when I heard the telltale knock at my door. I smiled grabbing two beers from the counter before letting my guest in.

"Welcome, friend," I said as I offered him a beer.

He came inside and accepted the beer. He held up a bottle of wine giving it a light shake. "For after."

I could feel his hidden innuendo. It was not a secret Arnie enjoyed the company of men. While I preferred the burning flesh of a woman, my vessel did not have any preference. So long as the blood ran red and thick on my fingers it really didn't matter. I was excited at the thought of what I planned to do to the unsuspecting pervert. It was okay if he mistook that excitement as interest. Let him think what he wanted for now. He would be educated well and good before the night was over.

"I was surprised you invited me over. The ladies said you were pretty much a recluse," Arnie commented looking around my home.

"What they call recluse I call selective," I replied with a sly smile.

The ladies were the female educators who had all but thrown themselves at me when I began my position at the school. In an institution field with so many women, the men found it necessary to ban together and bash them with no reason other than to promote their own masculinity. Those who were not already mated though they seemed to make their rounds within own their ranks. I was the newest male specimen and still a mystery to them all. That air of mystery brought them to me like moths to the sun.

"A man after my own heart," Arnie joked but I could see the question in his eyes. He wanted to know if I was a man after more than his heart. Perhaps I could have a bit of fun with my prey before dinner.

I took a long drag of my beer before smiling. "Heart? No. I was thinking a bit lower." *Entrails, more likely.*

I turned from him so he could not see my evil grin. I knew his jaw had dropped at my forwardness. These flesh bags all played such intrigues with each other. I found it much easier to be more forthcoming. It helped speed up getting to satisfying my urges. It also drew them to me so much more quickly than pretending to be elusive.

I moved to the kitchen counter placing my beer down. With the crook of my finger I beckoned him forward. He nearly dropped his beer as he hurried to me. We stood very close to each other, mere feet apart at that point. Arnie was leaning against the kitchen island taking a long drag of his beer. My eyes were drawn nearly closed feigning desire. I took his beer from him and let the cold liquid flow over my lips spilling down my chin wetting my neck.

"Oh my. What a mess I have made. However, will I clean all this up," I mocked.

Arnie didn't need any more invitation that than. He was on me, his lips slobbering over my own. His grubby hands tipped my head back as he licked the amber liquid from my skin. It wasn't long before his fingers were working open my jeans and he was on his knees servicing me. I took another long sip of his beer smiling. I pour some of the beer over my arousal letting him suction it from me. I didn't bother to look at him again until after I came to completion. While it didn't matter who was servicing me, I closed my eyes and pretended it was a more reluctant prey. Perhaps a whimpering helpless princess who had evaded me more times than I could count. I did recall though her seductive screams of pain as I had tortured her first with the fire blades and then with my own firm staff. I had spent many a night dreaming about repeating such glorious pleasures again and again. It was thoughts such as those that helped me finish with the mouth of another around me. It wasn't the lips I had wanted there but they did the trick, nonetheless. When I finally looked at him again, I could see some of my essence on his lips and chin.

"You have made me so very hungry now. Why don't you head into the bedroom and get undress so I can return the favor," I told me smiling pointing the way.

The man did not have to be asked twice. Arnie hurried into the bedroom disrobing as he went. I turned back to the counter running my fingers over the different types and sizes of blades in the holder. I picked one I felt would slice easily through Arnie's tough flesh. Moving eagerly into the bedroom, I still took my time. I wanted to savor the anticipation. I hadn't lied to him though. I was so very hungry, and the barbeque was ready for some flesh to burn.

Chapter 11

Nadine

 When I arrived back at the palace, I sought Danny out again. Guess where he was. You betcha. He was in the library browsing over scrolls. I pulled myself on the table next to him crossing my legs under me. I waited until he realized I was there. I smiled at his enthusiasm when he finally realized I had arrived. The man could be so engrossed sometimes I truly believed the apocalypse could be happening just outside the room and he would be none the wiser.

"Any news," I asked.

"Yes, actually. I was able to escape briefly from Josh's group therapy and break into the medical records area," he informed me.

That did not set well with me. Since Josh's therapy group was at the hospital, it was possible Lou had some of his minions stationed there. It was also the place where the coma patients had been stolen from. I didn't like him going to therapy alone as it was. Sneaking out of therapy for a solo mission put him in even more danger he was not trained for.

"Danny, that could have been dangerous," I scolded.

"Next time I will make sure to invite you. The opportunity arose and I had to take it. It was worth it though. I found out Xavier Jacobs had been a coma patient in the same hospital Josh had been committed to."

"That means he could very well be our demon."

"My thoughts exactly," Danny agreed.

That should have been good news, but it wasn't sitting well with me. Even though we may have identified Lou's vessel, we were still unsure how to get him out of it. Danny had been researching about how to approach the SLAGs about forcing a retraction. There were several entries about how others had dealt with the SLAG mindset but nowhere was anything about our current situation. The lore was scarce at best. The only information we had been able to gleam so far happened to be from Danny's friend, Vex.

Vex was once human but had long ago volunteered to be an emissary for the SLAGs for our world. The SLAGs did not speak our language. Their language was a series of clicks and grunts. Vex understood all of it though because he had been made into one of them, partly anyway. He was not of the hive mind as the SLAGs were known for. He was a hybrid, which made him different like me. He still had his human emotions, which the SLAGs felt was irrelevant. Emotions did not matter to the SLAGs, knowledge did. Knowledge and the balance of power.

"I am going to reach back out to my contact there again. Maybe he can offer some advice. It's all we have at this point," Danny told me.

I sighed feeling deflated. It didn't matter if we could prove Mr. Jacobs was Lou. Until we found a way to get him out of the vessel, I was stuck with him in the Real. At least I knew where he was though. It made me feel slightly better knowing what the bastard was up to. We could keep an eye on him at the very least.

The next day I was browsing the stack in the library looking for something to go along with my English report when I felt that sickly feeling again. Something not of that world was nearby again. It could have been minion or the dark master himself, but something was close. I could feel it. I pushed the book I had been holding back into the stack before turning back to the source of my uneasiness. The library was nearly empty. If they were going to attack it was as good of time as any. I prepared myself just in case. When I moved from the stacks, I found what was making me feel uneasy.

<u>Last of the Dream Warriors – Jealousy</u>

"Hello there, Miss Ruth. What a pleasure seeing you here this afternoon," Mr. Jacobs said in delight.

I didn't say anything back. I stood there staring at him and wondered how I had not noticed it sooner. The fractured slimy way he was jammed inside this vessel was practically screaming demon. Still, if I had not looked as closely as I was then I would not have noticed either. He had begun to blend into the body like I had been warned he would do.

I looked around me. He had me trapped in the stacks like an animal. His slickly sweet temperament made for a hard exit. He still didn't know I knew who he really was. I had to play it smart. We were not in the Realm after all. I couldn't just zap him out of existence as much as I really wanted to. I wouldn't be able to explain that away if I did. I still had to think of his vessel. The man was innocent, at least as far as I knew anyway.

"You seemed to have dropped this when you ran off in such a hurry the other day. I had hoped to see you in order to return it to you," he said holding out a piece of paper to me.

I didn't reach out for the paper and with good reason. The paper was stained pink in several areas. It was as if someone who had something very red on their hands had gripped it staining the white to pink. I didn't want to know how the paper was stained. I just wanted him gone but he was persistent. He waved the paper about as he continued his one-sided banter.

"I couldn't help but see you were writing your hypothesis on the true meaning behind dreams. It so happens I am an expert in the field of dreams. I could be a very good source of information. Perhaps we could meet after hours and I can show you my...research," he said moving closer to me.

I stepped back until I was almost at the end of the row. If he reached out, there was nothing I could do to stop him from harming me. I was much better at defending myself than I had been when last he attacked me. I also had my powers as a last resort. He didn't know that, and I was hesitant to use them. His vessel had over a hundred pounds on me and was in a position of authority. If I lashed out, he could have me suspended. That would leave all my friends and Danny alone with him in complete control. My options were limited.

"Thank you but no. I am fine with what I know already," I told him.

"That's very presumptuous of you. Don't be such a little princess. Take my advice and accept the offer," he demanded.

Had I any doubts before they had all been washed when he called me princess. His tone said it all. That was not Mr. Jacobs standing in front of me, not the real one anyway. It was Lou, my nemesis. It took all of me not to shudder in disgust. Instead, I let my anger be my guide.

"I don't take direction very well, but you should already know that. I think it's time we dropped the veil, don't you?"

His smile moved from happy to evil so subtly it would have been hard to catch unless you were looking right at him as I had been. Panic had made a home in me. I looked around trying to find some type of weapon to no avail. It would be hand to hand if he came at me. I knew if he forced my hand, I would end up using my powers. I had to get away from him before that happened. I could not be exposed.

"You are so right. Let's dropped the veil. You have something I want and planned to take it in spades."

Something he wanted? I was not sure what that I could be. My throne. My life. My world. All of them would be have been pretty good guesses. He had something more sinister in mind.

"I want your blood decorating my walls with such a pretty shade of red, princess. I won't be able to stand for anything less but first I want to know one thing. Who is the other traveler sent here to protect you," he told me.

He was looking for Danny. There was no way I would give up my friend without a fight. His threats aside, I would protect my friend at all costs. Before I could stop myself, my leg shot out hitting him with a direct shot between his legs. He crumpled under the force of the blow crying out. I gripped the shelves just above my head pulling myself up and over his hunched form. I didn't make it far though, just out of the stacks when I felt his nails digging into the flesh of my arm.

"I don't think so, little girl. You aren't going anywhere until I get my answers. Who is the other traveler," Mr. Jacobs growled at me digging his nails into my flesh.

"Is that really necessary," came a voice nearby.

We both looked to see Josh standing by the entrance, his arms tucked across his chest. He was leaning in a casual manner but nothing about him was casual. I knew he was ready to pounce, if necessary, to protect me. He was at war with what to do as much as I had been, but he didn't show it. Danny would give his life if need be to protect me. That was how he could lean so casual. He already made the decision before he uttered his first word.

"Daniel of Haasfolk."

"Josh, no. This doesn't concern you," I cried trying to keep up the pretense.

"It's okay, Nadine. He has had us made for a while now. Isn't that right, Soubackalou?"

Mr. Jacobs let go of my arm and squealed with glee. "Daniel, what a pleasant surprise. I must admit I did know it was either you or the James boy. After seeing how taken he is with our little princess here, I knew it couldn't be him. Anyone from our world wouldn't be so taken with the brat. My nephew excluded, of course, but we all know that apple didn't fall far from the rotten tree."

I moved closer to Josh and away from Mr. Jacobs. I tried not to let him bait me about AJ. It's what he wanted, and I couldn't play into his hands like that. I wasn't sure what he would do next, but I felt much safer closer to Josh than anywhere else in the room. Together, we could take him without my powers being revealed. Together we could be each other's alibi if things were to take a darker turn.

"I think it's time you left this place," Josh remarked in a firm voice.

"No. I don't think so. I think I will be sticking around here until I finished what I have started. Nice try though. I have to go but I will be seeing you two real soon. Don't you worry. I have plans for both of you I am sure you are going to love. Until then, children."

Lou left in a slow deliberate manner. Once he was gone both Josh and I took a collective breath. That had been a close one. Had Danny not come along I was not sure what would have happened. I could have fought Lou off but if I did the consequences either way would be devastating. I would either be kicked out of school leaving my friends to Lou's mercy or he would overpower me and torture me worse than he did the last time. It was a no-win situation. We needed the SLAGs to get on the same page as us and we needed it soon. My whole world depended on it.

"You should get to therapy. Miss Pauline will be looking for you. I will keep an eye out for him. Be safe," Danny said clasping my arm.

"You too. He is far too dangerous to let run free around here."

"Tell me something I don't know."

I was scared. I didn't say that to him, but I was thinking I was scared but more importantly mad. I was mad at creatures who had no emotions that were making determinations about my life, my world, without my input. It wasn't fair nor did it make sense. I knew Danny was doing everything he could to negotiate a solution. There had to be more I could be doing though. I felt helpless and vulnerable. That just made me angrier. One thing was for sure, Lou was not going to stop until he had blood on his hands and lots of it, preferably mine. I didn't think he would care though if he had to settle for second best. Danny needed as much protection as I did now. We had to keep each other's backs more now than ever.

Danny

Later that afternoon, I decided to walk the distance home. I was sorely lacking the cardio any decent warrior aspired to. Josh was not in too bad shape, even after a year in a coma. I needed to work my vessel's body out more if I planned to take on the Dark Lord with Nadine. After her little magical demonstration though, my thoughts were leaning toward her even needing me. If her powers were truly manifesting in the Real, I was more of a burden to her than anything else. She had enough to worry about without someone else she cared for having a target on their back.

I was coming to realize that I would never wish Nadine's life on anyone. She was the most powerful being I had ever heard of and believe me when I say I have read enough to know true power when I saw it. Still, Nadine was only human. She loved and lost just like any of us, probably even more so in her short life. Not only was she being hunted by a homicidal demonic manic, but she was battling her feelings for two different men. Both were the complete opposite of each other but were the same in one important way. They both seemed to care for my wayward friend. I saw her appeal with the ones she called friends though. I was glad to be counted among them.

It was these very thoughts I had rambling around my head when I noticed someone off in the distance. I was on guard. There were a number of possessed still about but the figure before me was not one of them. there had been scattered reports on the news channel about homeless men being accosted by men and women who barely spoke. The attackers, both men and women, had weird eyes and barely spoke English. I knew it was the coma patients that disappeared and were housing Lou's minions. The figure before me was not any of those poor souls though. It was actually the last person I had hoped to see. I sighed heavily knowing I could not stop this confrontation. I headed directly toward Carter stopping just in front of him.

"Why do I get the feeling you aren't here looking to give me a ride home," I asked sarcastically.

Carter looked at me with a hard glare before he ordered, "I want you to stay away from Nadine."

I felt for the guy. Truly, I did. The love of his life was drifting away from him and he had no idea why. He was on the defense in a battle of his own making and he thought I was the enemy. That was far from the truth but in his own juvenile mind I was competing for the love of his life. I truly did feel sorry for the clueless kid. It was not about Carter though or his misguided feelings. It was about protecting Nadine from a fate worse than death. It was about the Dark Lord. None of which I could say to him. All I could offer was this. "I am sorry, but I can't do that."

"She is my girlfriend," Carter argued.

The boy was frustrating me, but I remained in control. In my years of experience as a diplomat beside the king of Haasfolk, I had learned the meaning of patience. I needed to channel all the methods I had learned while talking with Carter. Nothing good would come from us coming to blows. I needed to keep it civil between us for Nadine. I understood why he felt as he did. I couldn't change the reality of things though. I could no more tell him the truth of things than Nadine could. Still, he had to be told the reality of the world.

"I know. So why don't you stop treating her like a possession," I offered.

That didn't seem to set well with Carter. He wanted to pick a fight. He wanted us to come to blows even after Nadine had asked him to be a bigger man. "You are screwing around with her, aren't you? Come on. You can tell me."

"First of all, I am not the type of guy who would kiss and tell, and I certainly wouldn't tell you if I was messing with her, which I am not. Second, don't you think you should be having this conversation with her since she is your girlfriend," I told him.

I was done with this conversation. We had bigger things to worry about than one boy's jealous streak. It was childish and I needed to be elsewhere. Still, Carter was not quite done with me yet.

"Ever since you got on the scene, I haven't been able to talk to her. She keeps things from me that I am pretty sure she is sharing with you," He argued.

I scoffed at that. I knew so much more than he would ever know about the depths of what Nadine had been keeping from him. I couldn't say that though. Still, I was done having my integrity put in doubt. I said as much. "She was keeping things from you before I was ever around so don't be blaming me for your disconnection."

"Does she talk to you about me? Huh? Is that it? Are you working on her by letting her pour her little heart out to you? Is that your game, Coma Boy?"

"You have no idea what you are talking about."

"Have you gotten in her pants yet? I bet you two talk about me while you are screwing. I bet you get a good laugh on how she is playing me," Carter urged.

I could not comprehend what Nadine actually saw in the boy. He really was looking for a reason to strike out at me. In a way, I could see his reasoning. Had Gloria been confiding in anyone other than me, I would probably feel just as hurt and angry as the boy in front of me. Still, I would not blame the confidant in the situation as it would have been Gloria's decision who she invited into her sphere. The conversation really was done now. I would not let him to continue to insult her purely because of his own insecurities. She deserved a lot better. She deserved someone worthy of her love. I really had no idea what Nadine saw in him. Whatever it was between them honesty was not one of those things. Honesty or trust. That was for sure. I was tired of Carter disrespecting my dear friend.

I grabbed Carter's shirt forms as I said, "Listen to me because I am only going to say this one time. Nadine loves you. Why is beyond me because you are the most jealous, pig-headed guy I have ever met. If you would lighten up on her. Stop giving her the third degree every time she talks to someone other than you or Kelly Ann. Maybe then she wouldn't be confiding in others about her problems."

"Did she tell you that," Carter asked shocked.

"She didn't have to. I have eyes. I can see her pain. Stop acting like the big tough guy and start being there for her or else you really will lose her to someone else."

Carter narrowed his eyes as he questioned, "Is that a threat?"

I let go of him sighing heavily. There was never getting through to such stubbornness even for a diplomatic like me. I knew a lost cause when I saw it. Carter wanted to blame everybody else for their problems when it was the loss of trust between the two of them that was killing their relationship, not me. I wasn't sure their relationship could last much longer at that point and I felt bad for my friend. I knew she really did love the boy.

"You know what? You don't even deserve her. Do you know that? She loves you and would do just about anything for you and you don't deserve any of it," I said before I walked away not looking back.

Carter was in Nadine's life by choice but that did not mean we had to be friends. I was there to defend her against the Dark Lord, not knuckleheads she intentionally kept in her life. I would do my job, no matter what Carter thought. If that meant Carter would be uncomfortable then so be it. I had a job to do and I was planning to do it to my fullest. Jealousy be damned.

Chapter 12

Nadine

The next day Kelly Ann found me sitting alone in the cafeteria. I had been trying to concentrate on my classwork, which had been slipping since Lou had decided to make an appearance. If I didn't buckle down, I would be in trouble. Not the life and death kind I was experiencing on a day to day basis, but still. I needed to keep my grades up and at least appear engaged while at the same time I battled for my life. If not, my grandmother would get wind of it and start pulling me from my other obligations. Not that I minded being removed from cheerleading, but I couldn't afford to be removed from Mr. Fong's. Who said high school was not hard enough already? So, when Kelly Ann sat next to me at the table, I was not ready for her drama, whatever it might be, and I told her as much.

"You haven't been in any kind of mood lately, girl. That is why I am here. We need to talk," She stated firmly.

"I am not going to get away with not going through this, am I," I questioned. Kelly Ann shook her head with a smirk. Yeah, I should have known better. I turned to her with a sigh as I conceded. "Okay. Fine. Let's do this then."

"Straight out there then. What is going on with you and Josh?"

"Josh?" Kelly Ann nodded. "Nothing. He is just a friend."

"Why does Carter think otherwise," She asked.

I was surprised she was bringing Josh up but then again not really. I mean she was my best friend and outside of the introduction to Sam in the last few years to our little group we were a pretty tight knit unit. That is until I began to dream and found out my dreams were really another world entirely. I knew she was here on behest of Carter. She wanted to know what was wrong between us. The truth was so much more complicated. Again, I would have to lie or deflect as I had been trained to do.

"I don't know. You might want to ask him," I said to her.

Kelly Ann folded her arms across her chest as she said, "I have."

"And?"

"And he says Josh is trying to get with you."

I scoffed at that. If they only knew the truth. Danny was married to my cousin and very much in love with her. There was no way he wanted to be with me in a romantic way. He was there to protect me and that was all. I couldn't tell Kelly Ann that though. I couldn't tell anyone that so instead I said, "That is crazy."

"I told him that too but then he started telling me all this stuff that doesn't make any sense," She said.

That made me curious. "Like what exactly?"

Kelly Ann recounted all my misdemeanors. I was spending way too much time alone with Josh and not nearly enough with my own boyfriend. I was ignoring calls and messages from my friends in favor of Josh. Most of all, I was keeping secrets from Carter and Kelly Ann about what we were doing together. My heart broke as she recounted that last one. All of it was true of course. The fact they knew I was keeping secrets from them hurt the most though. They knew something was wrong with the situation but had came to all the wrong conclusions because of all the secrets I had been keeping from them. That was my fault. Still, I had to deflect. I could not tell them the truth of things. Lives were already at stake, but they could never know that. In order to protect them I had to lie to them.

"The guy just came out of a coma. He doesn't remember who he used to be. All I am trying to do is make the guy feel less like a freak. Is that so hard to believe," I inserted trying not to break out into tears in front of her.

Kelly Ann sighed. Hugging me she said, "Nads, you have such a big heart sometimes that I worry people may try to take advantage of you. In the meantime, you are breaking Carter's heart by spending so much time with this guy."

"I am not cheating on Carter. I have told him as much until I am blue in the face. I love the big lug head," I stated firmly. And I wasn't cheating on Carter, not in the Real anyway. My dysfunctional relationship with AJ was not something I planned to even think about while Lou was stalking me in the Real. I didn't want to go there at all.

"I know you do, and I know you would never cheat on Carter."

"Then what are you trying to say to me," I asked confused.

Kelly Ann thought for a moment before saying, "I guess what I am trying to say is tread lightly. Our boy is hurting. It might be needlessly, but he still is hurting. Give him a break and spend some more time with him. I think that would save everyone a lot of heartache all around."

That was all I had ben doing lately, treading lightly. I had to with my friends and my family. I had to with the Council and everyone else in my life. Honestly, AJ had been the only one lately I didn't have to watch what I said around. He was a breath a fresh air in comparison. Perhaps I just didn't want to be his friend to help him but because he was helping me too. He helped me forget all the problems I had, even if it was just for a moment. It was that one moment that made all the difference.

It was thoughts of AJ running through my head and not about my dysfunctional relationship with Carter on my mind when I made my way back to the Realm that evening. I made my way to the training field wanting to get a session in before I headed out to see Guardian Riley when I found AJ training with Vega. They were not pulling any punches both giving as good as they got. It made me smile. I knew sometimes when sparring with Vega he had been pulling his punches, most likely because I was his princess. It did not look like Vega had the same fear of hurting AJ that he did with me. They were head to head, really into it.

When they were finished both men moved to the racks wiping the sweat from their faces. Vega waved to me with a smile, but AJ did not. In fact, he made great efforts not to look at me at all. I knew that was because I now knew who his relations were. I wasn't planning to hold it again him, but he was planning to be a bit more stubborn. I waited until Vega had started his laps before I approached AJ though so not to air all his dirty laundry to the world.

"You like spying on people I see," AJ said when I reached him.

"I didn't want to disturb you two while training. I was coming to practice with Cheswa. He wanted to see where my progress is at," I explained, not that I had to.

"So, they didn't send you to keep an eye on me," He inquired. The family. I figured I would be the last person they would send me to spy on anyone at that point, but I needed to make sure he understood that I came in peace with no agenda.

"No and even if they had asked me to, I wouldn't have."

AJ scoffed leaning in closer to me as he said, "Quite the little rebel you are. Why would you go against their wishes for the likes of me?"

"Because I do not believe they should treat you differently than anyone else. We are family and I want to be your friend," I said to him sincerely.

"You don't even know me," He argued.

"I know what I see. You might think you are a tough guy, but I think deep down inside you have a gentle heart."

"If you had any kind of sense you would stay far away from me like they said," he warned leaning even closer to me.

He was trying to intimidate me, and I won't lie. It was working a little. AJ was raw anger when he wanted to be. It was like lightning on an open wound. He wanted to push me away because he refused to believe there was any light inside him. It didn't matter to me who his uncle was. It didn't matter at all. What did matter was that he was so much better than what everyone was saying. He just had to see it for himself. I wanted to be the one to help him see that. God help me but I did.

"Is that what you want? For me to stay away from you?" He glared at me backing away slightly. I knew there was one way to get him to engage me. I smiled and picked up the staff left behind by Vega. I rotated the weight in my hand. "You know from the day I returned I have not had one person treat me like a human being, except maybe Danny that is. They all treat me like I am some fragile china doll who needs to have her feelings spared all while some monstrous dark lord is trying to kill me on like a regular basis. It's nuts." AJ squirms a bit at the mention of Lou. He gripped his staff tighter looking away. I knew then I had him. "It is really nice to have someone talk to me like I am some normal everyday person."

"I guess we both are the family freaks," AJ admitted.

"Something like that." I thought for a moment before continuing, "You don't have to fight with me, AJ. I am not like them."

He chuckled before saying, "And I should believe you because…"

I smiled knowing I really had him. I lifted my hand drawing my power. With a flick of my wrist, I used my powers to pull the staff from his hand and into my own. I stood there smiling with both staffs at the ready as I said, "Because I said so."

I could barely contain my laughter as I gazed upon his shocked expression.

"Hey," He cried looking from his empty hands to where his staff had landed.

"What? Did I catch you off guard," I mocked still smiling.

AJ moved to me ripping his staff from my hands with a huff before saying, "Only because I was not ready. If I had been you would never been able to take my staff from me."

That was where he was wrong. I was stronger than I looked by far. I planned to go easy on him though. I wanted to spar with him. I couldn't fathom why but it was all I really wanted to do in that moment. I wanted to be with AJ even if it was to spar. Call it my warrior instincts but I really, really wanted to spar with AJ.

"Wanna make a bet on that," I challenged him.

"Sure. What are the stakes," He asked smiling.

I shrugged, asking him what he felt the bet should be for. He smiled again giving me his mischievous grin before saying, "Never give the man that kind of opening. A guy like me might take advantage of you."

I told him I was tougher than I looked but he planned to test that theory. AJ came at me suddenly. He was trying to get me off guard as I had him. Our staffs met with a bang. My teeth almost chattered from the blow. Man, he was strong. I leaned closer over our connected staffs and asked what the terms of our bet were.

"To be determined," AJ stated smiling as he pushed back from me.

We sparred and as promised AJ showed me no mercy nor I him. For every move I made, he matched my own. We were well paired, and it showed. It was soon apparent we had gained an audience of Cheswa and some of the other training warriors. AJ was used to fighting in front of other, but I was not as used to it. Sure, I sparred almost daily with either Vega of Quintus, but the fields were usually pretty empty when he practiced. I was becoming self-conscious. AJ had found his opportunity and knocked me flat on my back by taking both my feet out from underneath me. I laid there for a moment catching my breath.

"You win," I conceded sitting up.

"Yeah but it was touch and go there for a while," He admitted surprisingly.

AJ extended his hand helping me up. I brushed off my clothes. He watched me curiously as if he was still trying to figure me out. I was just as an enigma to him as he was for me, I supposed. "You fought well."

"Thanks. So, did you," I told him.

He puffed out his chest proudly before saying, "No doubt."

The last few times I had been around AJ, the pull to be closer with him had been great. This time was no different. I didn't know what to say to him. I didn't know how to be around him. I think he could sense it as well because he too was at a loss for words.

"I should get to training with Cheswa before he thinks of some ingenious way of punishing me for being late."

AJ chuckled muttering, "Probably more laps."

I groaned loudly at the thought. I hated laps. It was nothing short of a lesser form of torture and that's coming from someone who had actually been tortured more than once in her life. Still it felt good, the banter between us. I didn't want it to end.

"So, I will see you around then," I asked hopefully.

"Definitely. I still have to cash in on that bet," he told me flashing that mischievous smile.

"I am probably going to regret this. Huh?"

AJ shrugged as he said, "You never know. See you around, rebel."

I watched him walk off before making my way over to Cheswa. Cheswa was Detoriolia's foremost battle trainer. His dwarf nature made for leathery skin and a big thick beard. What he didn't have in stature he made up for on the field. Cheswa made warriors out of all the young men and women who stepped onto the training fields. I was no different, even if I was a princess. We were a warrior race. I could not call myself their princess if I could not fight by the warriors' side as an equal.

When I stood in front of Cheswa I bowed my slightly as accustom when presenting to the battle trainer. It was several moments before he acknowledged me.

"Your man is a strong and full of fire," Cheswa stated.

I looked up at Cheswa confused as I said, "He is not my man. We are just friends." I shook off the confusion before adding, "He is practically family. His brother married my sister."

Cheswa folded his arms across his chest before saying, "I know who he is."

"Then why did you – "I began before he interrupted me.

"To see how you would react of, course. Everything is about reaction or have you not guessed that yet?" I looked at him shocked. Had I been so obvious? I didn't have a chance to think on it though because Cheswa was not one to waste any time. "Come. We need to fix the errors you made while sparring with your man."

He didn't wait for my response. He was already making his way down the field. I sighed not bothering to correct him again. Honestly, I was not even sure what AJ was to me anymore. I was curious about him though, more curious than I should be given I already had a boyfriend. I wasn't thinking about my issues with Carter though. In fact, Carter hadn't popped in my mind once while I was with AJ. Did that mean something? I wasn't sure. I wasn't ready to answer the question either. All I could think about was Kelly Ann had been right. I needed to figure things out. I needed to give Carter the attention he deserved. I just wasn't sure how I could do that with so much else going on. I didn't want to lie to him anymore, but I had no other choice. It wasn't just about me anymore. I had to protect Danny's identity as well. I had a whole world to protect from Lou and I knew I was doing a piss poor job of it. Still, I didn't know what more I could be doing. Things were definitely getting out of hand and I had no idea how to fix any of it. I pushed it all out of my head though. I had to train. I had to be a better warrior if I had any intentions of beating Lou at his own game.

Chapter 13

Nadine

Despite all the drama around what was happening in the Real, my family thought it was a good idea to have a party. Well, it wasn't just a party but a celebration of Antonio's birthday. Earlier in the week, I had visited one of the local tanners and precured a very nice pair of archer tabs and guards for him. Unicorn may rock the sword like no one I knew but Antonio was famous for his archery skills. I figured the tabs and guards were a safe bet. We presented him his gifts in a small gathering of just family and friends. It was actually nice to not have to be on point as we would have been with so many other people around. It was my family and a couple of the more weathered warriors under Antonio's command. Gloria was as stiff backed as ever but she was queen. That was just how she behaved, even with us.

I looked around to see if AJ was about when I entered the room. He had not officially made himself known as far I could tell to his brother or the rest of the family. He liked his anonymity and I could understand why he would not let them all know he was in Detoriola. They all did not think highly of him. it was a shame too because underneath all the gruff he was a pretty decent guy. that's what family did though. If they were not pushing you to do what they wanted, then they were not happy. Being attached to royalty made it that much harder for people like us.

I wondered if AJ had truly gone this time or if he might finally make his presence known. I wasn't sure which I preferred. It felt exciting to have him as my own little secret. Sure, Danny knew he was back too but that was only because I had told him. Vega knew too but he was not family. AJ had sought me out and not his own kin. That had to mean something. I was not sure how I felt about that. I did want it to mean something though, which was a concern in itself. I wanted to see him and yet I was afraid to see him again at the same time. AJ brought out things in me I was not ready to face, things I knew would have consequences I was really not ready for. I still wanted to see him though. it was frightening how much I wanted to see him.

"Do you think he will show," Danny asked bringing me a glass of champagne.

I shrugged taking the glass from him sipping slowly before saying, "It's his brother's birthday. It would not be right if he didn't."

"Well sometimes doing the wrong thing doesn't seem to stop some people."

I looked at Danny and knew he meant my odd relationship with AJ and the fact I was still seeing Carter I the Real. I sighed, not really having any defense for my actions. I love Carter, truly and deeply. Still, the lies between us had been weighing on our relationship, stressing it to the breaking point. AJ was just one more thing making me question our relationship. I could not deny my attraction to AJ. He was so full of life and understood me better than my own family. The new development about his family tree had been an issue for him but not for me. I wanted AJ in my life despite his relation to Lou. I just wasn't sure how much and in what way I could have him in my life.

"Not sure if this is a good thing or not but he just arrived," Danny told me, nodding in the direction behind me.

I turned around watching AJ clasps arms with his brother before bringing him in for a hug. They laughed about something. AJ seemed relatively happy, smiling in his banter with his brother. It wasn't until he spotted me staring that his smile waned. I wanted to wave or run to him, do something. Instead, I stood there like a statue staring at him. AJ tore his glance from me returning his attention to Antonio smiling again. I don't know why but I felt hurt to the point tears threatened to fall.

Danny placed a comforting hand on my shoulder before saying, "It is for the best."

"What is for the best and for who exactly," I questioned feeling my temper rising.

"You can't have them both, Nadine. It wouldn't be fair to either of them," Danny explained.

Danny was making some pretty big assumptions. Sure, I was confused about how I felt for AJ but besides a few nearly intimate moments, I had made myself very clear to AJ. We were meant to be friends. I was not available in that way to share myself with AJ. I had Carter and loved him. AJ was not for me and Danny knew that. Still, Danny saw more than most. Was I fooling no one but myself? I wondered if Danny was right.

"I just want to be AJ's friend," I whispered unable to look at anything but the floor.

"Are you sure that is all you really want out of this relationship," Danny asked.

That was the million-dollar question. What did I really want out of my relationship with AJ? I couldn't expect him to wait for me to decide what I wanted. I had been giving him mixed signals. If I was really interested in maintaining a true friendship with AJ, then I needed to be firm in my resolve. I couldn't let him kiss me and I most definitely couldn't engage in any more flirting. I had to keep it platonic. I just wasn't sure that was what I truly wanted.

Antonio, Unicorn and AJ had made their way over to us before I could voice a response to Danny. Antonio seemed to be beaming and why not. He had my sister wrapped around his arm and his brother by his side all celebrating his birthday. Much like his brother, Antonio's smile was infectious. He was happy to be in that moment with the people he loved. Antonio had no idea the angst brewing between me and AJ. He was just happy to be alive and with family.

"Look who graced us with his presence to celebrate my birth," Antonio cried out happily.

"Nadine, you remember AJ, Antonio's brother, right," Unicorn asked squeezing her husband's arm.

I looked at AJ then back to my sister. Oh yeah. I knew Antonio's brother. Probably better than any of them ever had. Then again, did any of us really know AJ? I was beginning to wonder that myself.

"Yes, we have met," I said, and Danny covered his mouth clearing his throat.

I looked at Danny briefly through narrowed eyes before plastering on my smile again giving my attention to the others. I would get him back later, probably at Mr. Fong's when I knock him out accidentally on purpose. Especially after Danny asked him, "How long do you think you will be visiting us this time around, AJ?"

"I am not sure. Things here haven't quite worked out as I expected. I might be taking off soon," AJ said without so much as a glance at me, but I knew the comment was directly related to me in every way.

"Your brother and our entire family will miss you," Unicorn said.

"Yes, you will be missed. I wish there was something we could do to make you stay. I think Detoriola has a lot to offer you," Danny said glancing at me with that knowing look.

I wasn't going to knock him out anymore. I was going to kill him.

"It is probably for the best I go," AJ offered sounding a bit sad about it.

"Well, we best finish making our way around to everyone. Enjoy the celebration," Antonio said moving off with Unicorn by his side and AJ in tow.

He hadn't looked at me, not once. Still, I didn't think AJ wanted to truly leave. I felt deep in me he was going because of me. Guilt was eating me up. I didn't want AJ to feel he couldn't be with his family because of me. We shared a family and would have to at the very least get along because of that. I had to make sure he knew I would not stand in his way of his relationship with his brother. I didn't want him to leave because of me.

I would get my chance to tell him just that much later in the evening. While the others were laughing and sharing drinks, I spotted AJ sneaking out the side entrance into the hall. I followed quickly calling out to him when I entered the hallway. He turned to me looking confused, his angry scowl had returned as well.

"What? What do you want," he barked.

"You're leaving? Just like that? You weren't even going to say good-bye or anything," I asked the pain in my voice shining through.

It hadn't occurred to me that I was in just as much pain as AJ over our situation. I was confused how I felt for him, but he was sure in his feelings. Despite my confused feelings though it hurt at the idea of him leaving. That meant something. I wasn't sure what but it did mean something. The last time I had left him, he seemed okay with how things were progressing with us. The time spent away from each other may have changed his feelings. Maybe he had cooled toward me. It hurt to think such a thing but perhaps it was for the best if that was the case. We were family after all. A civil relationship was better than nothing at all. Right?

"What reason do I have to stay," AJ asked making his way to me.

"You have your family. That should be enough."

"What if that isn't enough? What if I want more? What if what I want is so out of my reach that it would just hurt me to be around it if I stayed," he questioned.

He had me back against the wall from the momentum of his questioning. His frustration and fury were pouring out of him with every question until he looked down at me breathing hard. He wasn't talking about his family. He wasn't talking about the better life he wanted. He was talking about us. He was talking about wanting me and not being able to have me. He really did want me. In that moment there was nothing more I could want than him. Double life de damned. I wanted AJ. I couldn't help myself. I gave into the moment despite everything I told myself I would not do.

"You won't know what is out of your reach until you try and take it," I told him, knowing fully well what that meant.

His face was so close to mine our noses were touching as he said," If I do that I might not let go. I may never let go."

"Then don't," I whispered.

It was all the invitation he needed. His hands palmed the wall and his lips came crashing down on mine. My hands scrapped against his skull gripping his hair pulling him closer to me. I needed him closer, I wanted more. His hands slid off the wall. One cupped under me gripping my bottom. He pulled my leg up wrapping it around him as he held me closer. His body rubbed against mine sending fireworks through me. His mouth left mine sending wisps of kisses across my neck and shoulder. His other hand cupped my breast kneading it.

It wasn't until I could feel the physical expression of his need that I began second guessing what was happening. What was happening was wrong. I knew I shouldn't be there with him in such an intimate way. I wasn't free to give myself to anyone. It had nothing to do with any of the reasons you may think. I loved Carter. No matter how attracted I was to AJ, I was in love with someone else. My body was AJ's but my heart belonged to Carter. Letting AJ think any differently was wrong. I couldn't put that sort of pressure on me or him. I pushed AJ away taking several steps away from him.

"We can't do this. I can't do this," I told him catching my breath.

His look was filled with lust and anger. He balled his fists catching his breath as well. He shook his head violently after a moment and growled.

"I guess I was right. My family tree really does matter to you," he said through gritted teeth.

"What? That is not why we can't do this, AJ. I could careless who you are related to. I have a boyfriend who I love very much. That is the reason why we can only be friends," I corrected him.

"You don't care the Dark Lord is my uncle," he asked surprised. The revelation had taken him off guard to the point his anger all but nearly dissolved.

"You are not your family. I am not my family. We are our own people. We are people who can only be friends though."

He thought for a moment, and once he seemed resolved by the new course of action, he nodded as if in agreement. He began to walk past me as if going back into the ballroom. Just as he was about to pass though he grabbed me pushing me back against the wall again. His lips overtook mine with full fury and passion. I couldn't fight it; I was butter in his grasp. As quickly as the kiss began though it ended.

"Yeah. Just friends," he chuckled sarcastically before disappearing back in the room.

I took a moment to get a hold of myself. His kiss left a lasting effect on me I was scared to admit. I wanted to hit him at his audacity. The problem was I wanted to do more than hit him. I needed to stay away from him. There was no way I would be able to control the yearning inside me if he stayed in Detoriola. It was a good thing he wanted to go back to January. It was better if he left. The distance would be what was best. My issues with Lou and the Real were enough for now. I did not need my unwanted attraction with AJ added to the mix. He needed to return home.

Once I was able to return back to a semblance of normal, I headed back in the room. I made my way over to the buffet table and picked up a glass of Champagne still feeling a bit shaken by the encounter. I downed the glass in one gulp hoping it would settle my nerves. I needed something stronger than Champagne but had to make do with what we had. Danny made his way over to me as I picked up another flute. He could see I was flush and not just from the spirits.

"Care to share," he asked curiously.

I shook my head downing the next glass before slamming it back on the table. I turned in a huff to see AJ had found his brother again. They were talking intensely for a moment before both broke out into smiles. Antonio cheered hugged AJ tightly. Antonio then moved to the center of the room clinking his glass to get everyone's attention.

"Everyone, please. My brother has made me a very happy man today giving me the best gift by far. He has decided to finally take up our offer and make Detoriola his home, at least for the foreseeable future. Isn't that right, brother," Antonio announced.

"Yes. It is true. It turns out Detoriola has a lot to offer if you are willing to fight for it," AJ said staring right at me.

I stood there, shocked and unable to move. Danny moved beside me before whispering in my ear, "I wonder what ever could have changed his mind."

I couldn't give Danny the dirty look I wanted to. I couldn't move. AJ was staying in Detoriola and I was one hundred percent sure it was because of me. He had no intentions of honoring the fact I was with another man. He was the type of guy who played for keeps. His motivation was going to be so dangerous for me. Not just for my relationship with Carter but for my heart as well. I knew if I let him, I would fall for AJ hard. He was a gypsy by nature. I couldn't suffer the heart break of losing Carter and then possibly AJ as well. If AJ embraced his gypsy heritage he would leave eventually. When that happened, I would be in serious trouble.

Daniel

I was ill prepared for the day after such festivities as we had the night before. I ribbed Nadine about her relationship with AJ because we both believed he would be heading back to January soon enough. The revelation that he was staying in Detoriola for longer than anticipated had really hit home with Nadine. She insisted she only wanted to be AJ's friend. I knew she was only fooling herself, especially how disheveled she looked after their brief encounter at the party. Nadine had some turbulent times ahead of her and it had nothing to do with the Dark Lord. I wasn't sure how I could help her other than being there as her friend. I had to get my own mind straight if I was going to help her at all. The Real beckoned and we had a monster to hunt.

After the first period, I was standing talking with Sam when Miss Pauline sought me out. We were talking about music as it was when Miss Pauline made her way to us. I enjoyed soft melodies and what he called classical themes whereas Sam was a lover of the harder, more metal ballads. None of that mattered to Miss Pauline who was on a mission. She had that serious look on her face that I knew meant she was here in a more official role than normal. In my therapy sessions with her, Miss Pauline usually smiled and joked. She tried in every sense to make it feel like I was not being evaluated every time we spoke. That was not the demeanor she had today though. Something was amiss.

"Mr. Groves? I need to speak with you, Mr. Groves," she called.

"Of course, Miss Pauline. How can I help you," I asked trying to seem like a normal everyday teen Josh Groves should be.

Miss Pauline looked to Sam before saying, "Alone, if you do not mind."

I looked at Sam who shrugged. Despite being a bit different, Nadine's friends had embraced me. Well, that's not entirely true. They embraced me only when Carter was not around. It was like night and day how I was treated by everyone when Carter was around. I knew it was because of Nadine and Carter's barbaric claim to her. She may not admit it, but it was true. Everyone saw it but her. Sam had been a good friend though even when Carter was around. I knew he would be by my side if needed.

"I will catch you later, Sam, " I told him.

"Later, dude," he said with a salute to Miss Pauline before heading off.

"What can I do for you, Miss Pauline," I asked again.

"I was told you had detention last night with Mr. Anderson. Is that true," she asked.

I was a bit confused. I had heard about detention and what it entailed. The idea, while having its own merits, was not something that could work in the Realm. The Council was not known to put someone in a "time out". The closest thing to a "time out" would be the Void and anyone who knew better would say there was no comparison. I had not experienced detention yet as Miss Pauline was suggesting which confused me. I had been with Nadine the night before working on our research for who the Dark Lord could be. Not that I could relay that to her though.

"No. I did not have detention last evening."

Miss Pauline pulled out a time sheet and handed it to me before saying, "I have here that you and Miss Ruth were in detention room 3 with Mr. Anderson until four thirty. You were in detention because of three tardies in his class. Are you telling me that this record is incorrect?"

"I was not in detention last night with or without Nadine. I don't know where you got that information from but neither of us were in detention," I repeated firmly wondering where her information was coming from.

"I was told by the other teacher covering detention as well that you were there as well. What do you say about that," she said.

That had my warning signs way up. Who would tell her such a thing about me and why? I could feel the mark of the Dark Lord all over it. I wasn't sure why, but he had to be involved. I had to tread lightly to ensure I kept the unsuspecting teacher in my confidence. "Miss Pauline, I have no reason to lie. Why would I?"

"And you are saying this other party has a reason to lie," she countered.

I shrugged trying to remain calm and I was sure failing. I most certainly looked guilty even though I knew I was innocent. "I don't know why he told you I was there when I was not. I am sorry but I really was not there. I went home right after school yesterday. I swear."

Miss Pauline looked to think for a moment before saying, "Do you think Miss Ruth will collaborate your story?"

"I don't know what Nadine would say to you, but she definitely won't say I was in detention with her when I wasn't. That is for sure. What is all this about anyway?"

I could see the worry in her face. Something was amiss and it had to do with Mr. Anderson. I inquired as to what was happening. As it so happened, Mr. Anderson had gone missing. He had not showed up for work that day nor had he called out. He was not picking up his phone at home or his cell phone. He had simply vanished, and she was being told we were the last to see him alive. I was sure the last to see the missing teacher was the Dark Lord. Again, I could not offer that option to her.

"If this person said we had detention with him they were wrong and possibly they were the last person to see him last evening," I offered

Miss Pauline shook her head before saying, "I have no reason to doubt his word."

"But you have reason to doubt mine?"

Miss Pauline looked at me hard. She knew I was keeping things from her in our sessions, which always caused unneeded grief. Still, what was apparent could be taken at face value. Josh Groves was a model student and known element at the school. He had been popular before his accident. The educator the Dark Lord was pretending to be was not. He was still an educator though, nearly above reproach. Tough situation all around.

"I don't know. Should I? it's not like you have always been forthcoming with me, Josh."

I looked away from her unable to deal with the truth of the matter. I knew what Nadine was feeling in that way. I couldn't tell a counselor about my true self. Nadine could not tell the ones she loved her about her double life. Her pain was real on so many deeper levels than mine.

"Do you have something you want to tell me, Josh," Almost begging me to tell her the truth. "There isn't anything you can't tell me. I want to be there for you and for Nadine if she is involved. Please. Tell me what is going on."

I shook my head and with a firm voice confirmed I did not know where Mr. Anderson was. The Real was not my world. As much as I wished to have the dirty laundry aired, it was not my place. We were at an impasse.

"Perhaps I will just verify your story with Miss Ruth then," she said to me before heading off determined to get at the truth of things.

I hurried off in the direction I knew Nadine would be coming. Just as she was about to take her seat, Nadine spotted me. I waved at her frantically. She hurried to me looking back at the clock confused.

"Make it quick. Class is about to start," she told me.

"Watch out for Miss Pauline. She thinks we know something about Mr. Anderson's disappearance," I told her.

Nadine looked at me shocked before saying, "I didn't even know he was missing."

"Well he is, and she thinks we know what happened to him."

Nadine asked astonished, "Why would she think that?"

I told her what I knew and all she could do was nod. I could tell by the look on her face she had come to the same conclusion as I had. Someone was out to get us, and we didn't know who. The same Dark Lord who has manipulated his way into the Real was on the prowl. If Mr. Anderson was truly missing and Soubackalou was the last to see him it did not bode well for the teacher.

The bell rang overhead and Nadine ushered me away from the room. I needed to get to class and she needed to think about what she would say or do when Miss Pauline came for her. I knew Miss Pauline would come for her. The question was when.

Soubackalou

I watched Daniel posing as Josh run off to class. Miss Pauline came around the corner and I made sure I was in her way as to force a conversation with her. I had sent her on her merry way earlier with the tale I had concocted about the missing Mr. Anderson. I, of course knew where he was, or what was left of him anyway. I had been right. His meaty body had made for more than one meal over the week. Oh, how she would squeal if she knew I had some of the last reminisce of her dear fallen comrade in my lunch pail just inside my classroom. They were all so clueless, it was too amusing. Time to stoke the fires of doubt on the little princess and her little shadow.

I smiled and apologized for almost running Miss Pauline down. She of course accepted gracefully. She was too sweet for her own good. The inner beast inside me wanted to reach out and force her to the ground. She wouldn't be so forgiving when I ate her flesh from bone while it was still attached. I still needed her alive for now though. The mission came first though.

"So how goes your quest in finding Mr. Anderson? Any word or leads," I inquired trying my best to seem concerned.

"Not well. I have only spoken with Josh Groves so far and he denies even being in detention yesterday," Miss Pauline said then sighed in defeat.

"Really? What did he say?"

"Not much. He down and right denied being in detention despite the records on file from last night," she told me.

Good thing I was able to change the records for detention. I needed a patsy for my own naughty deeds. I figured I could kill two birds with one stone. "He is lying of course. I wonder why."

"I don't know but he did make a beeline to Nadine's class right after we spoke," She admitted.

I offered then, "Perhaps he is trying to protect Nadine. Teenage couples will do just about anything for each other."

Miss Pauline looked at me confused before saying, "I didn't know they were together. I would have sworn she was with Carter James."

I knew the girl was in counseling sessions from previous encounters with the luscious Miss Pauline. It made sense the little brat might have revealed her infatuations. I needed to reign the situation back into my favor, use what I knew to convince her that the princess and her friend were still very suspect. Both Daniel and the princess had been keeping secrets from everyone they knew in the Real. Their behavior was suspect and with a bit of a push I could implicate them in just about anything.

"Kids. They can never hold each other's fancy for very long. I would definitely investigate the protection angle though. They are both hiding something. I can feel it," I said throwing my hands up in the air trying to be more animated than necessary.

Miss Pauline nodded taking my words in as she said, "Perhaps you are right. I better get on with it."

"But of course. Don't let me stop you."

I watched her head down the hall to Nadine's class. I smiled as she pulled the princess to the side to have her confrontation. If I knew the princess, she would be anything but forthcoming. That was just one added layer of the things I had in place for her. I didn't wait to see where the conversation went. I already knew what would happen. Instead, I headed into my own class. I had another little piggy to look for. My vessel was getting hungry again and this time would not settle for old man meat. This time he wanted something young and tender. This time the prey needed to be someone that would hurt the princess where she called home. Choices, such choices I had before me. I just needed to decide on which would make the biggest impact.

Nadine

<u>Last of the Dream Warriors – Jealousy</u>

It was a good thing Danny was able to get to me before Miss Pauline. We needed to start getting a head of Lou's plans instead of being so reactionary to them. Danny and I were a team and he had given me the information I needed to be ready. I was prepared for her. I knew she would come for me soon. I hadn't expected so soon though. Miss Pauline interrupted class and I was excused to go with her. I stood outside my class and feigned confusion.

"I have to speak with you, Miss Ruth," she said sounding firmer than I had ever heard her.

"I am all ears, Miss Pauline. What's up," I said trying to sound chipper.

"I need to know where you were last night," she informed me.

"Well, after classes I went to Mr. Fong's Martial Arts Studio to help him with class and then from there I went home," I recounted for her.

"What time did you arrive at Mr. Fong's?"

"By four and I was there until nine. You can check with him if you like," I offered.

Miss Pauline looked confused as she said, "So you did not attend detention last night?"

She recalled the same story she told Josh to me. Someone had told her that Josh and I had detention with Mr. Anderson. If that was the case, then we would have been the last people to see Mr. Anderson alive. No one saw him leave the school. No one saw him on his way home, and he had been out of communication with everyone he knew since right before the end of school that day. We were her only lead.

"I would say the person who told you I saw him had the wrong person. That or someone is trying to cast suspicion at me where there is none, perhaps to draw it from themselves. Instead of interrogating students, you might want to start questioning the people he knew."

Miss Pauline was offended by that and made that known by saying "I am not trying to interrogate you, Nadine."

"Funny because that is what this feels like."

I didn't wait for her to say anything else to me. I turned on my heels and headed back to class. There was nothing left to say anyway. I was frustrated though. Lou was behind the missing teacher. I couldn't prove it, but I knew it to be true. I wasn't sure how to prove it since Miss Pauline had kept her source to herself. Another dead end. If we didn't figure out how to get him out of Mr. Jacobs, I wasn't sure what I was going to do. I knew one thing for certain. He was starting to bring his game to us. Things were going to escalate. It was only a matter of time now.

Chapter 14

The last thing I wanted to do was go to another party. One did not say no to Kelly Ann though. It was a welcomed distraction actually. I was still trying to figure out what Lou's game had been trying to incriminate me and Josh in the disappear of Mr. Anderson. I found it hard to believe that pinning a kidnapping on us was his ultimate goal. He was trying to cast a shadow over us with people in power. If he could convince the school Josh and I were that evil, no one would believe us when the truth about Mr. Jacobs came out. He was insidious and too dangerous for the Real. He was also brilliant when it came to his long-term game plans. This had been the first strike. I hated to think what else he had up his sleeve for us.

I planned to forget all about that for one evening though. I needed to reconnect with my friends and especially with Carter. These were the people I was fighting so hard to protect. I knew I had been neglecting them in my hunt for Lou. I wanted so badly to make up for keeping them all at a distance because of the Lou situation. I knocked on Kelly Ann's door expecting her to answer. I was happily surprised when it was Carter who met me at the door instead. As soon as he saw me, he lifted me up kissing me firmly, his arms squeezing me gently.

"Wow! What was that for," I asked after the kiss ended.

"Well, I missed you something fierce," he said to me snuggling closer.

I was guilt ridden for all the time we had lost over the last several weeks while I was chasing after Lou. "I missed you too, baby."

And I meant it. I really did miss the warmth I felt when I was with Carter. It was a comfort I didn't have with anyone else. Not even with AJ. There was something different between me and AJ that I was not ready to deal with. Now that he was staying in Detoriola I would eventually have to face him again though. I had a feeling if he has his way it would be sooner than later. I pushed the thought of AJ aside and concentrated on Carter though. He was my here and now. I didn't want to think about the bad that had happened or what was to come. I wanted to live for the moment with Carter. Who knew how many more moments like this we would have if Lou got his way? I wanted to cherish my time with Carter and my friends.

"What took you so long? I have been waiting forever for you to get here," he whined bringing me close to him again.

I giggled giving him a swat before saying, "I was studying late in the library."

"Alone?"

"Yes," I replied cautiously. Where was he going with this?

"So, no Coma Boy then?"

I sighed heavily shaking my head. "No. I haven't seen him all day for your information."

"Well, there is a first," Carter muttered.

I didn't like where this was going. I wanted it to be a pleasant evening, but it really got to me that Carter could not be more friendly with Josh. Danny was a great guy, one of the best I knew. He was a stranger in a strange land though. The person I counted on the most was treating Danny like competition when he was nothing of the sort. I was tired of having the same argument.

"Carter, I wish you would give him half a chance. He really is a nice guy if you get to know him."

"Maybe I will. I am sure he is here. After all, he has been spending more time with my girl than I have in the last few weeks. He is probably lurking nearby waiting for his chance to be in your space. Maybe he is waiting for you at work again. That was pleasant dropping you off to be with another guy."

"I told you before. He is helping me with my self-defense class," I reminded him trying not to raise my voice, but I was about at my wit's end with him.

"You never let me help but Coma Boy can. Why," He argued.

I didn't want to lie to Carter. I told him a semblance of what I knew to be true. Deflection as my beloved lost friend, Angelica, had taught me. "He finds it peaceful, if you must know."

Carter scoffed saying, "Peaceful? What the heck is peaceful about a bunch of kids punching and kicking each other?"

"Well, see that is it. They are kids. They don't know he is different from everyone else. You know, because of the coma and all. They accept him for who he is. To them, he isn't some freak like everyone at school has labeled him, my own boyfriend included," I informed him poking him lightly in the chest.

That seemed to make Carter think. It was not a lie either. Danny was used to warriors of all ages training in the fields just beyond the castle daily. It was a comfort to watch children of the Real practicing what the Detoriolians made into an art form. As Josh, Danny was different compared to those considered his peers there. Josh's old friends had abandoned him pretty early on when he took up hanging out with me. He was alone in a world who didn't accept him since he woke up. That had to change how Carter saw him, even slightly. Perhaps I was getting through that thick skull of Carter's though. I loved him but sometimes I really wanted to punch him. Kelly Ann told me plenty of times that was just how relationships were. I was beginning to think she was right.

"So, I am still your boyfriend then," Carter asked after a moment.

"There was some doubt that you weren't?"

He shrugged trying not to commit either way. The guilt was rearing its ugly head again. I was to blame for making him feel like that and I hated myself for it. I wasn't sure how I would ever make it up to him, but I was sure going to try. I just needed to get Lou out of the Real first. Everything relied on Lou no longer being an issue. Once he was gone everything could go back to normal or as normal as things could be when one lived a double life like me.

"Carter, I love you despite that hard head of yours. I know I haven't been around much for you lately, but I am going to work on that. Do you think you can do the same with Josh," I told him.

"You're my girl. I will do anything for you," he told me.

I kissed him lightly on the lips thanking him for agreeing to try. I let him wrap his arms around me holding me close to him. Carter's warmth was there waiting for me. There would be peace, at least for a little while. It was more than I could ask for. We made our way inside the party after a few more moments of just us. It was in full swing with music and laughter aplenty. It was good reconnecting with my friends after being so detached for so long. Even the cheerleaders were there, which was a surprise after the Ouija board incident over the summer. Melany was dancing with a guy I recognized from my Chem class. Lulu was nearby snickering at the mismatched couple with a few of her cronies. High school drama at its finest. It was what I missed. The past year had been murder on me. Even with the threat of Lou still out there, it was good to be reminded of what I was fighting for.

The evening progressed and I was finally beginning to feel like my old normal self again. It felt like ages since I had been allowed to just be me and not worry about anything but being a normal teenager. Just enjoying the company of my friends was something I missed dearly. Carter spent the evening close by chatting with our friends. Every so often he would sneak away from whomever he was talking with to find me and kiss me. Every time he did, I smiled holding on to him a moment more than the time before. It was during the last long hug I saw Josh enter the house looking about, in search of me no doubt.

I sighed letting Carter go. It had been a couple hours since I had to think about the dangers waiting for me outside Kelly Ann's house. I had no doubt Danny was planning to bring me back to reality. I watched Carter walk off again to refill his glass as Danny make his way through the crowd to me.

"You were supposed to meet me at Mr. Fong's," Danny said as he approached.

Had I said that? I was trying to remember earlier that day but was coming up a blank. Perhaps it was the beer in my hand. Perhaps it was just wishful thinking on my part. Either way, I had blocked out another evening of chasing my demons around, literally.

"I needed a night off, Danny," I said to him.

"Josh," he reminded me before adding, "You have responsibilities. Until they are wrapped up you don't get a night off. I was worried sick he got to you."

I felt a little guilty at that. It was a real possibility Lou could get to me as Mr. Jacobs. That was why he was here after all, to protect me from my nemesis. Still, if I gave up my entire life to chase Lou, if I gave into my fear, then what life would I have worth living? The Realm would have me on the throne giving up who I am to rule soon enough. This was my time to still be me. I didn't want that to go away, not just yet anyway.

"I am sorry. I should have told you," I conceded.

He nodded accepting my apology before adding, "Come on. I overheard Mr. Jacobs would be away for the evening. It's the perfect chance to see what he has hiding in his home."

Danny held out his hand expecting me to take it. He expected me to follow him blindly away from my life in the Real to chase after the life that invaded my sanctuary. I was not having it though. Not that night. I slapped his hand away before looping my arms across my chest.

"I told you I am taking the night off," I said standing my ground.

"I am serious, Nadine," he barked.

"And so am I. Every day and night I battle my demons. Tonight, I am not doing it. Tonight, I am hanging out with my friends and there is nothing you can do to stop me."

I know I sounded like spoiled child, but it was true. I was exhausted from all the worrying, training and utter nonsense. I really did need a night off. I needed to be a normal teenager, if only for one night.

Danny looked at me in disbelief. He really thought I would just up and leave me friends to go after Lou. Of course, he did. Every other time he asked I had in the last several weeks. My life had become about keeping our secret and stopping Lou. Life was about so much more though. That evening was just another a reminder of that.

"This is not fun and games, Nadine. I am leaving here right now, and I expect for you to come with me. This is not a negotiation," He ordered, his face starting to get red from anger.

"Have a good evening, Josh. I am staying right here," I told him just as serious.

He looked at me for a long moment brewing in silence. By that point, Carter had made his way back over to me. He kissed my cheek lightly before placing a resting arm around my shoulders. He turned to Josh and smiled.

"Hello, Josh. How's it hanging," Carter said offering the olive branch as promised.

Danny was not in a receiving mood though. The wheels were turning in his head. I could see it. He looked between me and Carter slowly. Danny's eyes narrowed.

"I hope you are happy. He is going to get you killed and you don't even care. He can see your weakness a mile away and will not hesitate to use it against you," Danny said pointing an angry finger at me.

Before I or Carter could say another word, Danny turned on his heels and walked out of the house. Carter scoffed before looking to me, "Does he think I plan on driving or something?"

"It doesn't matter," I muttered, silently cursing Danny for almost outing us with his little speech. Thankfully, Carter didn't understand the true meaning of his words. Danny had not been wrong but sometimes you just have to do what feels right. Being with Carter and my friends in that moment felt right.

"Can't say I didn't try," Carter commented shrugging his shoulders.

Danny's words sent a shiver down my spine, despite my resolve. He thought Lou would use Carter against me. Danny was probably right. Lou was a manipulative monster. He would use his charm and deception to tear my world apart. I couldn't let that happen, but I also couldn't let him control my life with fear. I needed to be me, the me I wanted to be, for as long as I could be. Danny may have been right, but I was not budging. I would do it my way. Danny would just have to accept that.

Chapter 15

Danny

The day went by quickly and I found myself again at Mr. Fong's with Nadine. We had not spoken much since our blow out at Kelly Ann's little gathering. Nadine had not sought me out in the Realm, nor had I looked for her either. I was still extremely angry with her. Lives were on the line and not just our own. She had become too distracted by petty issues with her friends. Her love life was a bigger distraction though. Her battling feelings for AJ and Carter were giving me a headache and I was just an innocent bystander. It was weighing on me keeping her secrets. I could only imagine what it was like for her. I sympathized but priorities had to be set.

I could feel Nadine's glare on me while I stretched. After a moment, I sighed and stood up facing her. "Do you wish to lecture me more or are we going to train?"

"I don't want to lecture you, Danny, and I don't expect one back. I just want to talk," she said trying to remain calm.

"When you talk it usually is in the form of lecturing me on your life here. You always seem to forget your duty to your kingdom. You know the place where you truly belong," I reminded her.

Nadine balled her fists as she said, "This is not the Realm. I have no kingdom here. I am just an ordinary girl trying to live an ordinary life."

I gave her that knowing look. "I think we both know you are far from ordinary," I scoffed.

"But I don't want to be anything but ordinary. Can't you see that?"

She was pleading with me to see things from her point of view. As a diplomat, I had been trained to do just that in situations less dire than the one we found ourselves in. She was right though. I was still a stranger in a very strange land. It had been hard enough learning how to act and be in the Real. I could only imagine what she had been going through the entire time since her true heritage had been revealed to her. It wasn't about us and our needs though. It was about something greater.

"I am not the only one you have to worry about here, Nadine. The Dark Lord has made it impossible for you to have the kind of life you want," I told her.

"He will be gone from here soon enough," Nadine said hopefully.

"And so, might you," I reminded her.

Nadine had a confused look on appear across her face. Her stature relaxed if only for a moment. I knew it wasn't the first time that it had been brought up. Her tether was the only thing keeping her in the Real. There was a good possibility the SLAG Nation would find a way to prevent her from travelling between worlds. It could happen sooner than later with the present situation as it was.

"You think when the SLAGs recall Lou that they might recall me as well," Nadine said as more a statement than a question.

"This is not your world. You have no real reason to stay here anymore. All this place is now is a distraction."

That seemed to set her off. "It is not a distraction. It is the only place I can remember as being home for me. It is all I have."

Perhaps, I was a bit offended. I was apart of the family Nadine was denying. I was married to her cousin. Gloria had given up so much in order to rule while everyone awaited Nadine's return. When she finally did, it became very apparent she was in no shape to rule. That forced Gloria to retain the throne for an unforeseen amount of time. That also meant my duties of ambassador for my homeland of Haasfolk had to be put on hold indefinitely. We had sacrificed so much for Nadine already and she had yet to return the favor. All she worried about was her precious few in the Real. I had finally had enough.

"This is not your home! Detoriola is your home. This place has been less of a home to you and more a prison. Look at the woman you call mother here. She holds you with such distain. The boy you call brother barely can take care of himself let alone care what happens to you. At home, you have a family who waits every evening for you to arrive home. What family do you have here?"

Nadine lowered her head and muttered, "I have Gillian and Sarah. They are my family too."

"Two old women who do not have long left in this world," I said unable to control myself. I regretted the moment the words left my lips.

Nadine gripped my shirt tightly. I waited for a blow that did not come. When I looked at her again, I could see she was trying to contain herself. I had hit a nerve. I apologized immediately. It was still a few moments before she released my shirt. She moved away from me still taking long deep breaths.

"Do not ever say anything bad about those two old women as you call them again. They mean more to me than anything in either worlds. They are my family no matter what you or anyone else says," she finally said.

"This can't be the life you want, Nadine. Always lying to your friends. You can never tell them who you really are. What kind of life is that?"

I was trying to make her see the truth for what it was. She had put so much in the Real and I could sympathize. In the short time I had been there, I too had become fond of the people who lived there. Still, the Realm was our home. The Real was only temporary for us both. She needed to see that.

"Is it," I pressed.

She turned to me and I could see the tears rimming her eyes. She pleaded with her stare for me to end my tirade. I knew it was cruel, but she had to see the truth. She had to admit it to herself if not to me. Her days in the Real were numbered.

"You can't keep turning away from the truth, Nadine. This world is not your home. Soon you will have to come to terms with that," I pressed harder.

"I don't think I am up to training tonight," she said unable to look at me.

I watched her leave, wishing I could follow. She needed to be with her own thoughts though. She needed to think it through. The Realm would always be there for her. It was her world. Her real family was there, and I would be there for her too. I knew leaving The Real would break her heart beyond anything I could ever imagine. It was inevitable though. All I could do was be there for her as her friend when it happened. A piece of me wished it wasn't so but even I knew better.

Nadine

I was still out of sorts from my conversation with Danny when I arrived back in the Realm. I knew I should be reporting for training. I didn't care though. I needed the evening off. I needed to be alone, away from the responsibilities of the crown. More importantly, I needed to be away from all the life and death situations that came with the crown. Princess or not, I was so tired of everything being so hard for me. I was a being hunted by a maniacal killer who was hell bent on stealing my throne. He had followed me into the one place I thought I was safe form him. There was nowhere safe for me now. Nowhere to lay down my guard. Well, no place but one I could think of.

I found myself in the chamber of the Power Crystal as if I had been drawn there. Its cool blue glow was the only illumination in the room, but it was enough. I sat by the platform where the Crystal hovered. It was already six feet tall on its own. The Crystal hovered above a glistening pond of liquid. I was told that the liquid was leavings that had dripped from the Crystal. The leavings were utilized by the Guardian and his apprentices to make healing orbs and dream weaving devices for those moving between the Realm and the Dreamscape.

I closed my eyes and sighed. The noise of life disappeared when I was in that room. It was a rare occasion I found myself alone in the chamber. Usually Riley was puttering about attempting to harness the power of the Crystal without ever being able to touch it. No human or demon alike could touch the Crystal without finding themselves in a pile of ash soon after. I felt kindred to the Crystal in that way. Everything I touched seemed to be turning to ash in front of me as well. My life had been far from perfect a year ago. At least before I ever found out about the Realm, I knew all my danger was of the human variety. If someone had told me a year ago that dreams were real and a demon halfling wanted me dead, I would have thought them in need of a stay in an asylum. Here I was though, in a living nightmare unable to tell those who mean the most to me about any of it.

"Such a long face for someone so miraculous. What troubles you, princess," came a caring voice.

When I opened my eyes, I found I was no longer alone. Guardian Riley was there with me standing only a few feet away, his slender hands tucked in his blue robes. Today his eyes were green again. I really have to ask him one day what that was all about. I had enough on my mind though. I sighed but made no move to leave. I wasn't ready to go back out into the world again, either worlds really.

"I needed some time away from my life," I explained to him.

He nodded as if he understood.

I had to wonder about that though. I knew no more about Riley than I did the guards I passed by to come inside the chamber. He was a mystery to me in almost every sense. I mean, I knew he was completely and utterly dedicated to his work. He took being the guardian very seriously. He was talented at healing and his eyes constantly changed color. Outside of that. I knew very little else about him.

"Could I ask you a question, Riley," I said crossing my arms over my knees.

He nodded again waving me on to ask.

"What was your life like before becoming Guardian?"

He thought for a moment before he joined me sitting by the Crystal. "I was living a fairly solitaire life tending the fields for my family when I was selected. I had shown great promise in my schooling as a healer for our village. When Guardian Regis was looking for his replacement, I was nominated by my people. It was a shock to us all that I was chosen. I have tried my best though to ensure that Guardian Regis's legacy and his choice was not in vain."

We spoke for a bit longer. He told me his village had been in Bock. It was one of the only ones with any type of vegetation there. I tried as hard as I might but could not recall Bock. I had been told of the great desert land but my memories of ever having visited such a place was still lost to me. It was one of those times I wished it wasn't though. I wished I could have a meaningful conversation with Riley about his homeland and not have to have him explain what he was talking about. Riley didn't make me feel different though because of my absentee memories. He instead found joy describing the sand dunes and beautiful oasis that could be found within the great desert land. It made me think of the Sahara the way he described it.

We were enjoying each other's company when suddenly the Power Crystal seemed to throb with energy. A huge drop of excess fell from the Crystal causing a large splash to occur. I felt the cool water hit me with no effect. Riley though seemed to have been burned by the substance. He leaped up with a cry as he rushed to tear off his outer robe. I stood as well trying to assist him the best I could. When the robe was off, I could see a heavy pink welt already appearing on Riley's arm where the robe had not protected him.

"Oh my god, Riley. Are you okay," I asked truly concerned for the man.

"Yes. I will be fine. It happens often when one works with such magic daily. How are you fairing? Did any get on you. Are you burned?"

His concern resonated with his voice. I checked myself over but found no burns or bruises from the waters that had splashed me. He could very well see the wet mark on my clothes from where I too had been splashed. I had not been injured though. I looked at him and shook my head. Instead of being satisfied, he looked even more concerned. It was not the first time my interaction with the magic from the Crystal was something that left him stumped.

"I should probably get going," I told him unable to handle the confused gaze any longer.

I didn't need him to say it. I was different. I knew that but it seemed more and more every day I had to face that fact over and over again. I was a child of prophecy, that was what they all whispered when they didn't think I could hear. It was about time I found out what that prophecy was.

It was not impossible to find the prophecies, but my family had made it pretty hard. The library in the palace alone was thousands of books. They were shelved in such a way only Danny could probably understand. That did not deter me though. I needed to know more about who everyone thought I was. Perhaps understanding how everyone saw me would help me understand the me they all knew, and I could not remember.

After about an hour of searching, I finally came upon it. The book was old, practically falling apart. I carefully removed the leather-bound book from the shelves and brought it to the large oak table where Danny and I had spent many hours studying. I flipped gently through the pages trying to find any mention of me. I knew my name would not grace the pages though, so I had to pay attention to the words. I found them after another hour or so of skimming pages.

> *A child born of passion will prepare for the throne. A grieving queen will find forbidden love with a man not destined to be her mate. The child conceived will know power unlike any the world had yet to see. The queen's life will be silenced by her own hands*

as she will not be able to contain the loss of her forbidden mate. She will succumb, leaving her kingdom unbalanced.

The child conceived will be a traveler of worlds, powerful in both beyond that which can be contained. The balance of both worlds will be left in the child's hands more than once. It remains unseen if the child will grow to be a force of good or evil. Strong willed and stubborn in nature her powers will change the course of the Realm as we know it.

There will be a battle unlike any the child will face. The battle will not only change the princess but change the Realm. It will change the Real. It will change everything. Many lives will be lost. Emerging from the beyond, it will be the child who will determine what the destiny of both worlds will be.

The prophecy. The thousands of years ago someone had peaked through time and that was what they saw. They saw my mother and her lover, who was not her betrothed. They saw her death. They saw me or what everyone believed to be me. Was the prophecy truly about me? Sure, I could fit myself into the circumstances, but did that mean it was really me? I was a traveler of worlds. I had powers no one could comprehend. To everyone, I could possibly be the child of prophesied about.

The prophecy spoke of a battle unlike any other I had faced yet. That sent a shiver down my spine. I had been through so much already. I couldn't fathom what more the Realm could throw at me. It would be in my power to change everything. I didn't like the sound of the last verse. What was this "beyond" the prophecy spoke of?

I want to find Danny or anyone in my family to ask them what it meant. I stopped myself though. I knew deep inside me they had just about as much insight as I did when it came to the prophecies written in that book. They were thousands of years old. Everything was left to interruption. Something was coming though. The Guardian had said it himself. Something was coming but he had no idea when. Many lives would be lost, and I had no idea how or what would be the cause. I could do nothing but let the prophecy unfold and hope I could stop the dangers that were heading our way.

Chapter 16

I planned to confront Lou on neutral territory. He could not come after me in the Real, not directly anyway. He needed to know that it was my world and he would not win at whatever game he was playing. He had stated plain enough that he had a plan for me and Danny. I was going to make it clear he would not win if he thought to play with us. The deck was most certainly stacked against him. Most of all, he needed to know he was on my turf. He was at my school, and these were my friends. It was my world. His games would not end well for him and he needed to know that.

I had rushed to stand outside of his classroom after the bells rung to do just that. Other students streamed passed me before he finally emerged from the classroom. When he saw me, he smiled. I could see the evil in him which made me sick. His happiness to see me knowing what we both knew made me sick. He really needed to get out of my world.

Leaning against the wall calmly he asked, "And what can I do for you, Miss Ruth?"

"You won't get away with whatever you are trying to do, Lou. I thought you should know that," I warned.

He chuckled before replying, "Giving me fair warning, eh? Then let me do the same. I hate to tell you but, in this world, I have the power, princess. I know your secret."

His confidence wasn't without warrant. He was right in some aspect. He was a teacher in my school and that could make for a very uncomfortable situation if he used that in his favor. He already alluded as much with the disappearance of Mr. Arnold. He tried to incite suspicion against Josh and I by falsifying records showing we were the last to see the missing teacher alive. Lucky for us though, I had an alibi. Mr. Fong could confirm my whereabouts, which in turn put a shadow of doubt over him. That plan had backfired, but I was sure he had many others brewing in that foul mind of his.

I looked around to see if anyone was nearby who I knew. I wanted to reply but wasn't going to get the chance. Carter had spotted me and was making his way toward us. That gave Lou the opportunity to put out one more dig. "I don't think you want me revealing what you really are to your friends. Do you?"

I opened my mouth to speak but Carter had arrived. He wrapped his arms around my waist kissing my cheek. He was oblivious to the fact my mortal enemy was standing nearby or that he had just interrupted a major confrontation. How could he know though? He didn't know my secret as Lou pointed out to eloquently.

"Hey baby. What's up," Carter asked.

"Nothing," I muttered still giving Lou a death stare.

"You two should be moving along. We all have class to attend," Lou said smiling behind the guise of Mr. Jacobs.

"On our way, sir," Carter replied reaching for my hand.

I took Carter's hand, trying not to scowl but losing that battle miserably. We left, much to my begrudgement since I had not had a chance to truly give Lou a piece of my mind. He was plotting something. I knew that. I just didn't know what. I had been hoping he would have incriminated himself in some slight way but never got the opportunity to get that far. I loved Carter but he was really starting to get in the way of figuring out what was Lou up to. I would have to try again later when Carter was not around.

Soubackalou

It was entertaining watching the little princess attempt to order me about as if she had any control what I did in the Real. I did know her secrets and had been able to utilize them for my own benefit. I needed to step up the game though. First and foremost, I needed to break her. That would start with her little clueless boyfriend. He needed to see her for what she truly was, a deceiver. I had not been sure until that moment on how to accomplish that though. Just as my prey was walking away from me, hand in hand with her boy toy, I spied something very interesting. Carter James had an admirer.

The girl was plain by most standards, but I could see a temptress in the making. Her red hair was pulled back in a tight braid. Fiery hair like that needed to be set free. Those spectacles needed to go as well. I had some work ahead of me but, if I was correct, the little vixen who was staring after the boy could be their downfall. She would need training. That much was for sure. I would have to clean my dwelling up a bit if I was to train her properly. One could not have body parts lying about with such fragile minds needing corruption. Still, the sacrifice would be worth the results. She would be a great work of hellish art when I was through with her. Introductions must be made first though, and I had the prefect plan.

It wasn't hard to find the little day dreamer's wet dream. I was impressed by the amount of detail she put into her Dreamscape. As I worked my way through a throng of half-naked oiled men, I found little Miss Barbara lounging across a golden throne being fed grapes by one of the beefy bodies. Another was massaging her exposed thighs. She wore slips of fabric over her body, which left nothing to the imagination. Well, to any normal man's imagination. I still wondered what her blood would look like as I rubbed it over my body. The bloodletting would have to wait though. I had an entirely different mission in mind for her.

I chuckled at the romance novel worthy depiction Barbara had brought to her fantasy. I would enjoy tantalizing the shrew so much more than I originally thought. With a wave of my hand and a squeeze of a stolen dream weaver, the beefy oiled worshippers disappeared. A shocked

<u>Last of the Dream Warriors – Jealousy</u>

Barbara sat up abruptly, looking about her. She then stood up looking at my angrily.

"Why are you still dressed? Where did my other slaves go," She barked. Ah, a spitfire! What fun this would be indeed.

I feigned a bow before righting myself and saying, "Dear queen, I dispatched them. I refuse to share you with anyone else."

"On your knees, slave," she ordered, pointing to a spot by her feet.

"I don't think so," I said chuckling.

"This is my dream. You will do what I command," She whined.

I moved passed her, taking the golden throne. I was owed a throne but for now that one would do. I lounged my legs over it before popping a single purple grape in my mouth. She looked furious. Her fists were balled at her side. Had the outfit been less ridiculous, I would almost feel sorry for her. Almost. Still, she needed to know who was boss if I was to train her properly. My vessel also had been craving more than the taste of human flesh lately. It wanted something I believed this slip of a girl could provide in troves.

"This is not just a simple dream, little queen, and I am not a simple slave willing to do your every bidding. I am here to help you though. Would you like to know how," I asked her.

She stared at me for a long moment before she asked, "Help me how?" Ah, yes. I had her interest. Now to reel her in.

I stood up, rubbing my hands together happily before saying, "I thought you would never ask. I know who you are, Barbara. I know the you the world sees, and I know the you that you could become if you let me help you."

In front of her, I willed a mirror gripping the weaver again. I showed her the frumpy little thing the Real saw her as. Her red hair tied in tight braids, big thick spectacles. She was what the children of the Real would call a nerd. Still, only I saw her true potential. I would make her see it as well. With a twirl of my wrist, the imagine changed and became the seductress I intended her to become. Gone were the glasses and braids. Her hair was loose and on was vibrant as if on fire. The frumpy clothes were gone leaving behind a beautiful black satin dress. Barbara stood there looking at her mirror imagine with her hand draped across her mouth in shock. She could be the girl in the mirror easily. I could make her that but first, she would have to offer herself to me completely. The girl knew a bargain when she saw one. I knew she would make the decision I wanted her to. All I had to do was reel her in.

"You want this," I said in barely a whisper.

"Please. Whatever it takes. I want to be that girl," she begged on hands and knees by my feet.

I grinned victoriously as I said, "I will hold you to that, dear. When you wake, I will need you to make yourself known to someone. This person will assist you in making the mirror image a reality. Do as he say explicitly, and you will have all your heart's desire."

I stood behind her, watching her staring at herself in the mirror. I didn't lay hands on her even though I wanted to badly. It would not be the same touching her flesh in the Real, but I needed her to rely on her own personal guardian angel. Little did she know I was demon born and in no way the angel she sought. I couldn't wait until she made herself known to my vessel. Training her would be such a thrill.

It didn't take Barbara long to arrive at my doorstep eagerly awaiting her transformation when she returned to the Real. I was aroused just thinking of all the dirty nasty things I would train her to do. I took my time answering the door, savoring our first introduction. She stood there in all her pig tailed glory, looking shy and not knowing what to say. I smiled at her innocence. I would break her from that shyness soon enough.

"Hello there. I believe we have a mutual friend who said you might be stopping by today. Do come in," I said to her.

She hurried in the house. I locked the door behind her and sat in my armchair watching her stand there uncomfortably. I let her stew under my stare for a good five minutes before said another word. She hadn't moved nor looked at me since she entered. She was waiting for me to tell her what to do. Good obedient little minion. It would be so much fun training her.

"In order to determine what I am working with I will need you to disrobe," I told her.

She looked like a frightened child, shaking at the thought of showing me her naked self. That would not do. I needed the temptress I knew she could be. I needed her to believe in herself. I would have to break her down to build her up. We were short on time otherwise I would savor such an idea. I needed to get my plans moving though. No time for savoring the break.

I huffed crossing my legs as I said, "You need to be more comfortable with the body you have been given. It is your palate and I will be your artist. In this place there should be no secrets between us. Let me see what you have been hiding from the world."

She moved her hands to the buttons of her shirt but paused. I smiled as she was waiting for my permission. Such a good little servant. I waved her on. She sighed heavily and turned from me. She removed every inch of her clothes. Using her arms and hands, she tried to cover her most delicate parts. She turned back to me with her eyes closed. She looked to be on the verge of crying. Her fear and pain excited me. I stood and began to disrobe as I circled her, my prey. Once fully disrobed, I stood before her. I could feel her fear emanating off her and I was immediately aroused.

Lifting her chin so I could see her eyes I said, "I will teach you how to not just please a man but yourself. I will give you to the tools to make men want you with the power of your body. "

I reached out and grabbed her hand. I placed it over my arousal. She tried to pull away, but I stopped her. I moved her hand over it back and forth bringing myself to fruition. My seed escaped the tiny distance between us landing against her pale skin. I growled still hungry for more.

"That is the power you have over men. Don't let them lie to you when they say it is about love. All men want sex, Barbara. You have the power to have them crave it from you. You have the power to take it from them. Do you want me to show you more," I asked her.

She looked at my full firm body and nodded biting her lip. I had tempted her as the snake had tempted Eve in the garden so long ago. Our game would end as tragic for her. Before the tragic end though, I would have so much fun. She was, after all, an eager student. I would train her well before I released her on her intended victim. I would equip her with every trick known to man and demon so she could seduce the one I knew she truly wanted. Her goals aligned happily with mine. If all went to plan, I wasn't just going to ruin the princess's relationship with her family but everyone in the Real. It would all start with her loving, jealous and very frustrating boyfriend, Carter James. First, I had to plant the seeds of doubt.

It was not hard to find the boy. He had been at a local hangout that some of the mass liked to entertain. The young ones anyway. I found him sitting by a pool table with some friends. Strait laced as he seemed, he was not sporting any spirits but only a single bottle of water. Such a good boy. We would have to change that, my pet and me.

I neared him with one purpose in mind. I was there to sow the seeds of doubt in his relationship with my little prey. I took the spirits I was pretending to partake, and made my way around the room greeting my oh too eager students. I circled the room with false smiles and happy interludes. When I came to Carter and his friends, they shared the same greetings as the rest. I lingered there though, watching the couple Carter had been with fawning over each other oblivious to those around them.

"They seem like a happy couple," I commented.

"Sam and Kelly Ann have been together for a while," Carter offered.

"Where is your lady love this evening? Should she not be here with you as well," I asked, pitching my first volley.

Carter shrugged, looking a bit more tense than he was before I came over. Ah! The sore spot I wanted. Now to test the wound. "Oh, that's right. I saw Miss Ruth and Mr. Groves outside that little gym on my way over here this evening looking very comfortable with each other. I was surprised I didn't see you with them. I thought you two were a couple."

"We are," Carter stated firmly.

"Oh. I am sorry. If I said something out of turn. You kids are young. Its hard to keep track of who is seeing who nowadays."

"They are just working," Carter explained, but I was sure it was more to try to convince himself more than me.

"If you say so," I said, sipping my drink and trying not to show my glee at the boy's distress.

Carter stewed for several moments before apologizing. He hurried from the establishment in pursuit, I was sure, of his lady love. I took my time following, slowly. I found the boy standing outside the building looking sadly inside the window. I approached slowly not to startle my prey. Spying inside, I could see Nadine and her companion laughing. They were sparring and having a good way to go with it. Perfect for my needs as it were.

"She has been blowing you off all week and look where she is now. She is spending time with that boy laughing and rolling about. You are not a thought in her head," I whispered in his ear.

"There is a good reason for all this. There has to be," he tried to reason but was failing miserably.

"What other explanation could there be?"

"She is helping Josh. That's all." He sounded as if he was trying to convince himself more than me. I knew the truth of course. They were kin and because of that merely friends. The boy was there trying to protect the princess from me. It was laughable of course but the truth of it all the same. Still, Carter knew none of it. He knew nothing of the princess's true identity. The veil of deception they needed to keep up worked so well in my favor. It helped cast the doubt I needed to cause in order to bring a divide between the princess and her friends. I dug the wedge deeper.

"What about you though? Don't you need her just as much? She used to give you all her time but no more. Not since the coma boy came into her life though. All there has been is secrets between you two since he came into your lives," I pressed him.

"She loves me. I know it," he finally said after a moment.

I had him and I knew it. His doubt in her had festered long before I came to the Real. She had made things that much easier to corrupt. It was so simple to just sow even more seeds of doubt in him. The boy was crying out for her love, but she was too busy trying to stop me to return his love. I didn't have to do much at all to break their relationship. All I needed to do was point out the obvious.

"Sometimes love just isn't enough."

I stood back, watching the boy's anger build. He squeezed his fist around the water bottle he was still carrying. After a moment, he heaved it at the window before stalking off angrily. Mission accomplished. Once my training was complete with the little red headed vixen, I would completely sever the ties of their relationship. Barbara would reel him in and give him something to help his broken heart. Something that would tear the couple apart undoubtably. Once that was accomplished, I would be one step closer to claiming my prey both here and in the Realm.

Chapter 17

Nadine

Was that Carter with Lou outside the studio? I was a bit freaked out. There had been a bang at the window and I only briefly caught the sight of someone walking away. I know I definitely saw Lou standing out there. He lingered far longer than the other person who had hurried off. It couldn't have been Carter though. He was planning to spend the evening out with Kelly Ann and Sam at the pool hall. He knew I was working and typically never came to the studio when I was. It couldn't have been Carter. Still whoever it was looked freakishly like him. Whoever it had been looked to have stomped off angry. What was Lou's game?

"Are we done for the evening," Danny asked, still catching his breath. Danny hadn't seen them, and I decided not to bother him with it.

Danny had been doing better in his training but still lacked the stamina of a true warrior. He was keeping up and with a foe like Lou out there he needed to be able to. We all did. I didn't want to underestimate Lou any more than I had already. Him showing up at the studio reminded me of that fact.

"Sure. I need to get home and hit the books now. I am starting to fall behind," I told him.

Starting to fall behind was an understatement but I didn't want to panic my overly educated friend. Danny had taken to high school like a thirsty horse was drawn to water. He was doing better than me at that point and had taken to helping me with my studies...again. Both teacher for me in the Realm as well as the Real now. Still, I had one thing on him. I could throw a mean right hook. At least in that area he had not excelled over me, not yet anyway.

"Do you want me to come over and simplify it for you," Danny asked sincerely.

I shook my head before adding, "I think you would be better served doing a bit of recon on the Dark Lord." I didn't tell him about the visit, but someone needed to check out what he was up to being so close to the studio.

He nodded, gathering up his gear. He looked to be in deep thought. I hesitated in asking what was on his mind though. We had spent the last few weeks arguing over my time spent in the Real and the choices I had been making. I didn't want another flare up again between us. He was not just my ally in our war with Lou but also a good friend. I hated fighting with him over things that were mostly out of my control. Still, I valued his opinion and regardless of what he thought I was listening.

"Will I be seeing you this evening for review then," Danny asked tossing his gear over his shoulder. He meant in the Realm.

I shrugged, not wanting to commit to more schooling. I was really done for the day but there was still so much more for me to learn in both worlds. I was getting tired of burning the candle at both ends though. A girl just wants a night off every once and a while. Once I was crowned, I would no longer have the freedoms I did now. I wanted to covet the freedom I had in both worlds for a bit longer.

"Will you be seeing AJ this evening instead," he inquired.

I sighed. AJ was an issue I was not ready to deal with. My feelings for him were not waning and that was a problem. I wanted to be the friendly face he saw when dealing with the family. Instead, I had let our mutual attraction get in the way of that. Not to mention the guilt I was feeling about him when it came to Carter. I was in essence betraying my boyfriend with another man. It didn't matter if he was a world away, literally. It was still a betrayal. As much as I wanted to stay away from AJ though, I found myself drawn to him like no other. I wasn't sure why, but I had no control when he was around.

"I was hoping for a quiet night," I told him.

"Does that ever work out for you," he said with a chuckle.

No. It never seemed to, but a girl had to try, right? Perhaps if I hid away from the world for a while, I could figure out what to do with my lives. There was one thing I had been curious about lately. IT had been creeping up on me slowly but with so much going on my mind had been elsewhere. I had been thinking about it a lot since the loss of my child. Diana. She was my first born but I had spent little time getting to know her since my return. I wasn't sure if that was by design or purely coincidence. I thought it was time to get to know my child better though. Maybe she could help me with my current dilemma as well.

I made the decision that my evening would be spent getting to know Diana better. Danny and I left the studio and I made my way home. I didn't waste any time. Our workout had exhausted me as it was, so I was able to fall asleep right away. As soon as I arrived at the palace, I went in search of Diana. I found her tending to a garden just inside the palace walls.

Diana, in all her poise, was sporting a floral dress which was a mismatch for the large garden gloves and hat had on. She was kneeling on a mat as she pruned and weeded. That was a complete surprise to me. I had no clue to what Diana did when she was not worrying over the state of the kingdom. I would never have fathomed a guess she was gardening.

The garden has been my mother's. She too had loved to tend it when she was in deep thought thinking over matters of the kingdom. That I had been told anyway. I had not spent much time with my mother before her untimely demise. Untimely demise. A nice way of saying suicide. She took herself from us because of her own selfish desires. I couldn't help but feel kindred with her in the sense that we both were taken from our children at very young ages because of our own actions. I, at least, had time and means to make a manse for what I had done in my youth. My mother, not so much.

"Mind if I join you," I asked, interrupting Diana's peaceful evening.

"You never have to ask, mother. Please do," she said as she gracefully stood.

We sat on the bench near the garden together. She daintily removed her gloves before folding her hands on her lap. "What can I do for you?"

I wasn't sure where to being. How does one go about learning more about the child they weren't there for when she grew up?

Diana actually looked a few years older than me than the other way around. She would have most likely taken the throne months ago had I not returned from the Real when I did. She had grown up being bred for such a thing. Looking at her, I could see the refinement a princess of such caliber should have. I was in no way that princess, but Diana was. She was more royal than I could ever be. I wondered if I had been around to raise her would the same still hold true. It was an odd situation all around.

"I wanted to spend some time with you," I admitted.

Her face blushed over as she said, "I have wanted that as well."

"Then why haven't we done this before," I asked her curiously.

She sighed, looking away from me. I knew then the answer without being told. My sister and cousin had decided and so it was. There had been many times during my return that they had knowingly kept things from me for what they felt was for my own good or the overall greater good. A lot had been done lately for my own good without ever asking me if I thought it was something I even wanted. They had been worried about my memories returning, or more importantly, the old me returning. I understood their concern, but I couldn't see how getting to know my own daughter would be a bad thing.

"It's okay. I get it. Everyone has been trying to deal with me with kid gloves. I wish for once they would see that I am not the same girl who was sent away so long ago," I told her honestly.

"They are only doing what they think is best, mother. We can not fault them for that," Diana said, diplomatically.

"You are my child. I will never understand them keeping you at a distance from me, especially after -" I couldn't continue. It still hurt thinking about the loss of my other child, especially at the hands of Lou.

Diana hugged me, knowing instinctively it was exactly what I needed. It felt right hugging her as I guessed it should since she was my only living child after all. I had lost one child, but I very much still had one alive and well, no thanks to me. I could never wrap my head around why I would let the Council and my family send me away into the Real when I had a child to think about. Diana would not hold those answers for me though. Those answers were still locked away in my lost memories and no idea how to trigger them to return. That evening was not supposed to be about me and my swiss cheese memories though. It was about my daughter.

"So, you like to garden," I asked, curious and wanting to get to know her more.

"This is the only place in the palace I have been able to find where I can be at one with my thoughts. It is a calming place," she told me.

I could see that. There were a number of blooms in the garden surrounding the outer wall. In middle of it all was a beautiful fountain with a veiled woman holding her hands to the sky. It was a popular theme I had seen throughout the kingdom, especially in the Belgrino Gardens.

The veiled woman was supposed to be the infamous woman in white, Wysteria. Her story seemed to go hand in hand with that of Lord Evil. He had been a man once but through corruption and wizardry he became the dark being known as Lord Evil we all knew. When Lord Evil had just beginning to wreak havoc on the world, the woman in white came to the Guardian and gave him gifts to beat back the monstrosity Lord Evil had become. No one was sure if he could be killed but he had been stopped, at least for the time being. He was always lurking about though using his Dark Lords for his insidious works. Lou was no different. He was the favorite of his master.

"I wish I had such a place of my own. Especially nowadays," I told her.

"You may share this place with me if you like, mother. After all, one day this will all be yours anyway to do with as you please."

"Right. Once I stop traveling uncontrollably between worlds and am not being hunted for my life, I get to have throne to look forward to," I said sarcastically.

She looked at me and asked curiously, "Do you not want the throne?"

"It's not that I don't want it. I don't think I am ready to give up my life for it," I admitted.

And that was true. I would have to give up everything to be queen. I would no longer have the freedom I did now. I would need to be the essence of propriety as well as an example for the whole kingdom. I was barely passing high school but soon I would be forced to rule a whole kingdom. Not just any kingdom though. Detoriola was the first kingdom and home of the Power Crystal. I faced a life of never-ending war and politicians vying for control. It was not something I looked forward to.

"You are a Princess of Detoriola whether you sit on the throne or not. You always have been. This is your life and you should embrace it. The reason you have such turmoil is because you are fighting what is meant to be," she told me plainly.

She was right. I had been fighting who I was supposed to be but then again who made the decision of who I was supposed to be? I know I had not. I was not included in the decision of how my life should unfold. That was what set me on edge. My whole life had been plotted out for me and no one bothered to ask me what I wanted. Not my family nor the Council had asked me what I wanted. They all assumed I would just fall into line with what they said was right. I wasn't ready to do that though. That had been what I learned. It was one of the foremost reasons I had been sent away in the first place. I refused to conform back then, and I was still not conforming to their wishes. Back then, it was because I had been defiant. Now it was because I truly did not understand the customs of my home world. All of it was the obligations I refused to take up before had vanished with my memories. I did not know what I did not know, and it was seen as defiance.

"Where I come from people get to choose their own path in life. This one was thrust upon me." I told her.

"You come from Detoriola. I understand you may not remember this world but what I say is true. The Real is not your home."

And that was the crux of my issues. I could not wrap my head around what she said, not entirely. The Realm was my home but for me it was still a new world. I could only recall fleeting memories of my life there before I was sent away. Everything I really knew was from the Real. That was my home too. Everyone wanted me to give up the only place I could truly remember being a part of. I couldn't do it though. Giving up the Real was like giving up a part of myself. I could never ask anyone do that for me. I was aggravated they were asking me to do just that for them.

"Daniel has told me he feels your relationships in the Real are what hold you from leaving that place for good. That you travel there still because unconsciously you fear giving up those you care about there. From what I have seen, I think he may be right," Diana informed me.

Danny thought my feelings for my family and friends in the Real was the reason I continued to travel between worlds. That made a bit of sense. I was bonded to my friends in a way I had never been with anyone in the Realm. Not that I could recall anyway. I loved them more than anything in either worlds. The fear of leaving them could be what was behind what kept me from staying grounded to the Realm. I wondered if Danny shared that revelation with Gloria and my sister. I wondered what else was on his mind he was keeping from me.

"The boy you wish to be your mate in particular," Diana added after a moment. She as talking about Carter.

"I love Carter very much. I don't know what I would do if I lost him," I told her honestly.

Diana held my hand with a sigh as she said, "If you love him as you say, how is it you can have such affections with AJ?" I sat back shocked. Had we been that obvious or did Danny have looser lips than I thought? Diana quickly added seeing my shock, "The others do not know. I saw you both in the hallway at the reception and figured it out all on my own."

"I am not sure what is happening with AJ. I wanted to be his friend but -" I was unable to finish. To finish would be to admit what I didn't want to face. There were a lot of things I was not ready to face.

"But you are attracted to him," she finished for me. "This attraction contradicts your feelings for Carter, and you are confused."

"You're good. Its like you can see right through me," I told her, both proud and sad at the same time.

If she could see through me so well, I was scared how long it would take the others to see as well. Diana had been trained from birth though to observe people and their behavior. She had been raised to be a diplomat. She was a good one at that. So had my cousin though. Did Gloria see through me so easily as Diana had?

"What will you do about the conflict," She asked instead of acknowledging the compliment.

"I have no clue. Any ideas," I asked with a slight chuckle.

Diana had none to offer. It would a conflict of interest for her to help me chose either way. If she agreed I should continue with my relationship with Carter and ignore the attraction to AJ, she feared of losing me to the Real for good, if that was even possible. If she told me I should choose AJ, it might show her preference to have me bound only to the Realm again. She would then have her mother back for more than a few hours every evening. That would be selfish on her part, so she didn't offer it up no matter how much she wanted it to be so. It wouldn't matter any way. I needed to figure it out on my own. I just had no idea what I was doing or how to decide. All I knew was that I loved Carter. No matter what was brewing between me and AJ, I was sure of that. AJ was a million miles and a world away, literally, from us and I intended to keep it that way. The rest would eventually sort itself out. I could not imagine life without Carter. For that reason alone, I planned to keep it platonic as possibly with AJ. It was possible to just be friends with someone you had a strange attraction to, right?

Chapter 18

Soubackalou

The delicious naked plaything stretched seductively in my bed. I knew her intent but kept my distance for a reason. Tonight, she would graduate on to the playing board. I had spent many wonderful hours honing her seductive powers for one intention, to break the bond between my prey and her would-be mate. Barbara had been so eager to learn that it did not matter what I threw at her. She took what I gave her and was ever hungry for more. She took to her training even more when I added some very stocky and curious other bedfellows. It was all for her education and she was a master pupil. Barbara was ready, for that I was sure. That evening would be our last encounter together before I sent her into the game ready to take down my fleshy obstacle. Because it would be our last encounter, I had something devilishly naughty for her in mind.

"Has my precious rested thoroughly enough this evening," I asked her.

She purred in response stretching like a devious kitten.

"Good. Why don't you come into the living room and see what I have brought you," I said, offering her my hand.

She swept herself up, her fiery locks flowing wildly as I liked them. Taking my hand, I led her into the living room. There sat four burly looking young sailors. They had been harassing a poor wee thing down at a local dive when I happened across them. They had been intentionally brutal with the girl because pain was their game. That I could understand and I even could relate. They had let me voyeur their brutality and it was then I knew I had the prefect graduation gift for my precious plaything. After many hours shaping my little vixen, I found pain was also her game as well. It would be a fun evening.

I stepped behind her letting her know without mistake how excited I was to see her surprise at the gift I brought her. I rested my hands on her shoulders, my lips just grazing her ear. "Tomorrow you start your mission and fulfil your every desire. Tonight, you will fulfil mine."

She gasped surprised by my gift to her. The gasp sent a thrill not just through me but all the studs waiting to mount my little filly. They were eager and I knew she would not disappoint. I gently pushed her down to her knees with no resistance. I motioned for the first two sweaty sailors to come for her and have their way with her. Two men I had found were not a problem for my little vixen. Four would be a fun sight to witness.

Tonight, would be for me but tomorrow I would turn my little creation lose on the world. My groundwork had been laid out. Carter James was ready for someone to give him the attention he had been missing from the distracted little princess. I would ruin every relationship she had before I finally took her life. There was nothing she could do to stop me, and the best part was she was making it so easy to ruin her life.

I watched the two sailors penetrating Barbara with ease. Ecstasy was written all over her face. I smiled inviting the other two over to partake in the pleasure of her as well. She had a busy night ahead of her with so many to pleasure. I would give her time to rest afterwards though because the real fun would begin tomorrow night.

Nadine

I had spent the rest of the evening alone after I took my leave from Diana. I had much to contemplate from our brief encounter. She had given me a lot to think about after all. Diana was a lot like Danny. I could see why he would take to her for a confiding ear. I had been more of a problem than a friend lately to him and I was regretting that. Still, I had no way of how to fix the issue. Lou had placed me in a very precarious position as it was and Danny was the only one who was seeing things from both sides, both worlds. He was hardly impartial though and made that very clear. Danny had tried to seem as if he was even with his treatment of both worlds but in reality, he was bias in favor of the Realm. It made sense. The Realm had always been his home. He had always known who he was and what he wanted to be in life. He had a choice whereas I never did. Not in the Realm anyway. In the Real, I still had choices, still had my free will. I was not bound to anything or anyone, certainly not a throne. Those I chose to bind myself to were my choice. My family had no say in that.

I guess that was what it all came down to. My family in the Realm vs my friends in the Real. There was a choice I would eventually have to make. I was unsure if I would even be given the choice. I knew deep down inside me my family would not let me give up the Realm, even if I could. Even if I knew how to, my family would never let me go. Instead of feeling love for them because of that, I felt frustration. In truth though, they were right. The Real was not my true home. Had I not been sent there in the first place my friends would not be in danger. I had caused all the heartbreak and sorrow Carter was feeling every time I chose Josh over him. I was the reason he was so unhappy. If I never came to the Real, Carter could have fell in love with someone more worthy of his love. Instead, I threw it away each day I lied to him, each day I thought of another man a world away.

AJ was not the problem. I was. AJ was just another reason showing me why I didn't belong in the Real. I did not belong in the Real. They all said it, but it was AJ that made me actually feel it. I was attracted to him because he was from my world. He was a path I was most likely meant to take. I was attracted to him because he was the choice I should be making. Still, my heart was too filled with Carter to completely give myself to AJ as I should. My heart was Carter's and the Real, but I belonged to the Realm. I always belonged to the Realm. The Real had only been meant to be a pit stop, a hiding place while my family dealt with the threat of Lou. Had I not lost my memories perhaps things would have been different. Perhaps my heart would belong to another in the Realm. Maybe Diana's father, who I still could not remember.

Where was he anyway, Diana's father? Why did he stay away when I returned from the Real? Why did he let me sacrifice myself for him when I was sent away? What type of man would let the mother of his child face inquiry and banishment to save himself? All those questions and more I had for him. Ultimately, I knew though it was my choice. It had always been my choice. I made the choice to protect Diana's father and I was the one who let the Council banish me to the Real. It was my actions that lead to all the heartache my family and friends felt. I was the problem and I had no idea how to find the solution.

I wished more than anything Fuller was still alive. Sure, I should be craving my mother or the company of my living family. It was Fuller though who had been with me through it all. He knew the girl I once was and helped me grown into the one I became. He was there when I had no father. He was there when I had no mother or, in Lily's case, lack of a caring one. Fuller had found love in the Real much as I had. He understood what it was like loving someone who he could never truly be with. Gillian and Fuller lived as husband and wife for over 15 years with his secret hanging over his head. Their relationship was different than mine and Carter's though. Gillian had trusted Fuller wholeheartedly. She only knew him as her husband and no other. Carter didn't trust me as Gillian did Fuller. I had given him ample reason not to though.

"You look so downtrodden. What ails you, sister," came a voice breaking my internal flogging.

I looked to my sister who was standing in my doorway. She was staring at me curiously. Unicorn understood physical things. She could get behind fighting out an issue easily. The turmoil inside me though was not so easily dispatched.

"It is nothing you need worry about. I am – I will be fine," I corrected myself.

"Perhaps I can assist?"

That was Unicorn. For as long as I could remember (which isn't far with my swiss cheese memories actually) she was always trying to protect me. My first memory was of our mother telling her to do just that. As an obedient princess, Unicorn followed our mother's request to the letter. She, in a way, became the mother I never knew. We were only separated by a handful of years, but she was my mother in all ways that counted.

<u>Last of the Dream Warriors – Jealousy</u>

"Just in need of a vacation from my life," I told her with a sigh.

Unicorn nodded in a knowing way.

That made me wonder. Did my sister ever want to be more than her station? Did she ever not want to be commander of the Detoriolian armies? What would my sister's life had been like if I had not been born? I was the reason our family, our kingdom, was at war with Lou. Had my mother not fell in love with my father things would have been very different for Detoriola. Another princess, a darker one, would be on the throne. The Power Crystal would be in control my evil. My birth, as much of blight as it was on my family, did stop the Dark Lord's end game. If all else, that was something good out of my conception. Still my birth and turbulent youth had caused many pains to my family. My life was still causing heart break to them all.

"Once the Dark Lord is out of the Real perhaps things can back to normal once more," Unicorn suggested.

Back to normal. I had to scoff at the idea. My life was anything but normal. Still, I would settle for Lou out of the Real and back in the Realm where he belonged. I could consider him only hunting me in the Realm as normal. It was as normal as I could hope for anyway. Lou would not give up trying to steal my throne though. He wanted the throne in order to gain access to the Power Crystal. It didn't matter that he could not touch it. As long as he could control those who could harness its power, he would be satisfied. There was no way I was going to let that happen. I had to stop him but first and foremost I had to get him out of the Real and away from my friends before someone I cared about got hurt.

Soubackalou

Sated. That was how I felt, utterly sated. Though my demented little soul was still craving a much larger target, Barbara had been a wonderfully wicked student. She had taken on those four sailors satisfying all their darkest desires before bringing me to completion as well. The lovely welts on her freshly pink skin would fade in a day or so. My vessel had wanted blood but knew we still needed her for our overall goal. We settled for the pretty shade of pink left on her skin from the rough hands and stiff belts of our guests.

"Have I graduated, master," she asked me from her throne upon my lap where she sat, me still stiff inside her.

I gripped her arms tightly behind her, forcing her down as I finished. Yes, she had graduated nicely. I had many things planned for her, all things she would love. The rift between the princess and her wayward boy toy was growing deeper each day. Barbara would use the skills I had taught her to drive a defining final wedge between them. From there, I would begin a systematic assault on everything she held dear. I had refrained from hunting children on school property though so not to call too much attention to myself. All that would change now that Barbara was ready. With the princess's attention drawn toward my actions, she would be driven more and more away from her friends. By the time I was finished, the prickly little princess would be utterly alone and I would strike my final blow. The little chit would never know what hit her.

Chapter 19

Carter

I was getting really sick and tired of Nadine blowing me off for Josh. I tried to be understanding but that only went so far. As it was, I barely saw her anymore. If it was not for school, I might not see her at all. She spent all her free time either in cheer or at Mr. Fong's. Guess who signed up to be a helper at Mr. Fong's after school as well. You got it! Coma freaking boy, Josh. I was kicking myself for not thinking about signing up as well. Mr. Fong didn't need any more additional help though. He had Nadine and Josh. Ugh! I hated to even say his name. Why couldn't he keep with his old crowd? Why did he need to be a part of our group?

It was pathetic, I know, but I had started following them around. I had to spy on my own freaking girlfriend just to get even close to her anymore. I was angry at how much time she was dedicating to him. I was furious at how easily she laughed at his jokes. Those laughs belonged to me. She belonged to me and he was stealing her away. She may not have realized it or ever admit it, but he was. There was absolutely nothing I could do about it. The more I tried to fight it, the more he was able to dig in deeper with her. I was reaching my breaking point and nothing good would come if I didn't find a way to get him out of our lives for good.

I gave myself the night off of self-torture and headed over to the pool hall. Perhaps a few games of pool mixed with a few drinks and I would feel better about the situation. Tonight, I would not be settling for water though. I needed something to dull my nerves and I knew Mitch would hook me up. Mitch was the brother of the owner and had no bones about providing spirits to the underage. I didn't recognize the few people around except good ole Mitch when I entered the pool hall set on my purpose. He didn't mind serving minors, but he didn't make a habit of it. When he saw I was fit to be tied, Mitch handed me a fresh cold beer and pointed me to an open table. I racked the table set on playing a solo round until something better came along. I was shocked to hear the clink of quarters so soon. When I looked up, I found a somewhat familiar face from school.

It was Barbara from my Chem class. She was usually very strait laced with her hair tied back in pigtails and glasses round on her face. She had always been shy. I had known her only because she once tutored me in Algebra. The person before me though was Barbara but not the one I recognized. The girl before me was wearing a leather skirt that barely hid her bottom. That girl had her long red locks flowing around her. Gone were her coke bottle glasses. That Barbara was dangerously hot, and she wanted to play pool with me.

"Looking for a game," she questioned, running her fingers along her pool stick.

"You can break," I told her, grabbing my pool stick.

She smiled seductively at me and bent slowly over the table in front of me. Her already short skirt gave me a peek of the barely their fabric between her legs. I looked away gripping my pool stick a little tighter. She was hot and she knew it. She was playing more than pool with me. I should have just gotten up and left but it felt good to be wanted, even if it was by someone other than my girlfriend. We were only playing pool anyway, no matter what Barbara thought. If Nadine could laugh with Coma Boy then I could most certainly play pool with another girl.

Barbara broke. One of the striped balls found its mark. She turned to me pursing her lips in a smile. I cleared my throat pushing back the attraction I was feeling as I said, "Guess that makes me solid."

Barbara reached the little distance between us cupping me between my legs giving me a little squeeze before stating, "Really solid."

Barbara was definitely wanting to play more than pool though. I pulled away from her, grabbing my beer. With one gulp, I downed the thing, wiping my mouth with the back of my hand. I looked at her again seeing her still smiling seductively at me. She turned her attention back to the table sinking in her next two balls before finally missing one. I was happy it was my turn because every time she made a move, I got more familiar with her version of Victoria's Secret. It didn't help every time she took a shot, I had to down a beer. I didn't want to admit it, but it was affecting me more than it should, the beer and the girl.

"You know. I was surprised to see you here all alone tonight," Barbara commented as I tried to figure out my first shot.

"Yeah why is that," I said, not looking at her but at the table.

"Well aren't you usually here with your friends. You know. Sam, Kelly ann and Nancy."

"Nadine. Her name is Nadine," I muttered.

I knew Barbara knew Nadine's name. I had been friends with Nadine long before we became an item. Barbara knew that as well. She was up to something. Perhaps it was just to tease but I wasn't sure I was into her game. The alcohol I had already consumed wanted to see how the game played out though. It was not like I had anything better to do anyway. After all, Nadine had blown me off again to be at the studio with Coma Boy again.

"Oh. That's right. Isn't she the girl everyone is talking about? I mean she's the one who is 'helping' josh Groves recoup right," she said, happily using the quotes when she reached that word which completely irked me.

I hadn't meant to, but I ended up growling just a bit.

She frowned moving next to me. She placed a light hand on my shoulder before saying, "Seems like I hit a nerve. Do you want to talk about it?"

I looked at her, really looked at her. She had always been a smart girl. Had I not been in love with Nadine, Barbara may have been someone I could have gotten close to. Looking at her full breasts just hovering inches from my face made me wonder why I hadn't noticed her before today. She wanted me to confide in her but I wasn't ready to admit my failure with Nadine to myself let alone someone else. I put down my stick standing in front of her.

"Not really. It's nothing," I said, trying to convince myself more than her.

"It's not nothing if it is bothering you that your girlfriend is spending time with another guy. Have you talked to her about it?"

I couldn't believe I was having that conversation. I sat down at one of the high tables nearby, gulping down yet another beer. I was on five at least, possibly six. I had not drunk that much since my sister's 21st birthday. That had been over a year ago when things between me and Nadine were last solid. I was feeling the happy buzz of alcohol in my veins. I shook my head, fighting back the burning anger inside me.

"You know what I think," she said, inching closer to me with each word. "I think if it is good for the goose its good for the gander. If Nadine can spend all her time with another guy, then maybe you should think about spending some time with other girls."

I shook my head again, fighting off the cloud of confusion the alcohol was fogging my brain with. "I love Nadine."

"No one is saying you don't. All I am suggesting is that you keep your options open. Perhaps you might run into someone who is willing to satisfy some of those needs she hasn't or isn't willing to."

Her hands ran up my thighs, nails scraping my jean clad things until she was positioned right between my legs. Her hands touched my chest and I won't lie to you. It felt good. It felt heavenly to be touched by someone who wanted me. It was someone who wanted me with no strings attached. It was a seductive feeling. Still, I loved Nadine. I couldn't believe I even thought for a moment about betraying her. I gripped Barbara's wrist holding them at her sides.

"I don't have feelings for you like that," I told her firmly.

She smiled leaning against me until her mouth touched my ear. "We don't need emotions. I want you to just feel this."

Her hand took mine and placed it between her legs. I could feel the silk mesh between her legs and her excited warmth. I could feel what was under those panties. I was ashamed to admit it, but it excited me to feel her so intimately. She was giving me free access to her with no assurances from me. She wanted me and that was enough for her. She wasn't holding back because she wasn't ready. She wasn't running to be with another guy. She was there with me and giving me intimate access to her. There was no lie between us, only desire.

"More than your hand wants to be between my legs. I want to give you a night you will never forget. I think you want that too. If you do, I live just down the street. I will meet you there If you want me to show you what you have been missing. I suggest you don't wait too long, or I will have to start without you," she whispered in my ear.

She slid a key into my hand before sashaying her way out the door. My eyes were glued to her backside as it swayed out the door. I shifted in my seat telling my little friend to calm down as I gulped down yet another beer. I motioned to Mitch for another, but he gave me the cut off signal. I wiped my mouth from the excess again still looking toward the door where Barbara had left through. I then looked down at the key in my hand. I hadn't even realized I had been squeezing it until that moment. I knew I would probably regret the decision when I sobered up but in that moment I didn't care. I needed to feel wanted by someone, anyone. I followed after Barbara damning myself the entire way.

I woke unsure at first where I was, but I knew one thing for sure. My head was killing me. I was in a strange room naked except the blanket wrapped around me. I tried remembering what happened but was drawing a blank. It didn't occur to me anything was really wrong until two hands came around me. One handheld a glass of water, the other two aspirin. I took them with a groan.

"I knew you might need a little assistance this morning. You were really throwing them back last night," a voice behind me whispered gleefully in my ear.

<u>Last of the Dream Warriors – Jealousy</u>

I muttered a thanks. It was all coming back to me. Barbara, the pool hall, after the pool hall. I had done the worst thing imaginable. I did the thing I accused Nadine of doing. I cheated on her with Barbara. I didn't just cheat though. I enjoyed it.

"Looks like you need my help again with that big problem of yours. Don't worry. I will get you to school on time. That is, if you really want to go," Barbara whispered seductively in my ear as her hands roamed my body.

Her hand disappeared under the blanket finding its prize and my eyes rolled back in my head with a moan. She moved herself on my lap and I found she had not bothered dressing yet either. Barbara pushed me back on the bed with a greedy smile.

"Don't worry, Carter. I am going to make all those cloudy thoughts fly away. You just lie back and enjoy it," she told me.

The amount of shame I was feeling had been eclipsed by need. I needed what she was willing to give. I needed unconditional affection and Barbara was giving it away in spades. When her mouth wrapped around my arousal, I knew we weren't going to make it to school on time. I had no idea what I was going to say to Nadine when I saw her again, but it didn't matter. Nothing else mattered but what I was feeling in that moment. I would deal with the shame of my betrayal later, much later.

It wasn't until way past first period Barbara and I finally emerged from her apartment. She had promised what we had done would only be between us and if I ever had the need, she would be there for me. She reaffirmed that by giving me the key again she had presented me with the night before. I was riddled with shame but took it quickly before making my way to school. I didn't see any of the others until lunch, which was a good thing. I knew one look at me, and they would all know something was amiss, especially Nadine. She was really good at reading me. I figured even if she did notice something though she wouldn't get into it with me in front of her precious Coma Boy.

Josh. It was all his fault. If Coma Boy had not woken up, then Barbara would never had happened. Nadine's time would have been spent with me and Barbara would have never been an option. Drinking had not helped. I could blame Josh or the booze all I wanted though but the truth was I let myself fall into Barbara's seductive hands. I had not needed any help.

Nadine found me as soon as I sat down on the bench with my bagged lunch. Yeah, Barbara made me lunch too. I hadn't the appetite to even see what it was though. Eating Barbara's food in front of Nadine seemed wrong. It seemed even more intimate than all the things we had done together the night before. I tossed it in the nearest trash can unable to even look at the bag.

"Hey! Where have you been? I waited for over an hour this morning. I thought you were picking me up," Nadine inquired, hugging me.

Guilt swept through my body. I had forgotten I was supposed to pick her up before school. Damn. I had no excuse planned and had no idea what to say to her. I had also missed precious time with her I wouldn't be able to get back. I shrugged trying to be as noncommitting as possible. I didn't want to lie but I definitely could not tell her the truth. She wasn't about to let it go though.

"I called the house and everything. Your sister said you didn't come home last night. Did you spend the night at the lot?"

My father's car lot. It was a place we both had spent many a night trying to distance ourselves from our volatile families. Had she just given me an alibi? I shrugged again not committing to the story but letting her think whatever excuse she would come up with. That brought a look I had not seen in a while from her. Was its sympathy? Understanding? I was not sure, but she bought the story she created for me. It made me feel even worse that she trusted me so much she could create me an alibi and believe it so easily. I had been so suspicious of her with Josh and she believed in me so much. I was a terrible, horrible boyfriend.

"Jesus, Carter. I wish you would have let me know. I would have come out for a little while and joined you. I miss hanging at the lot with you."

God but I missed that too. I missed how we had been before we became a couple. No, that's not entirely true. I missed the time when we first became a couple. The feelings of how new and yet familiar we were for each other. Ever since her grandfather passed away though things had been on a steady decline between us. We were being pulled apart by unknown forces.

"I am sorry," I muttered.

And I was sorry. I was sorry for the lie now between us. I was sorry I had let us fall so far away from each other that straying had become possible. Most importantly, I was sorry there was nothing I could do to fix the problems between us because I was not the only one at fault. For months Nadine had been avoiding telling me the truth about a lot of things. She had been keeping secrets from me and admitted as much. Now I had a secret, but I had no plan of admitting mine though. Until Nadine was completely honest with me, we would both have our secrets to keep.

Chapter 20

Soubackalou

My vessel had a craving and it was becoming overwhelming. I needed to feed its need or else I would not be focused on the game at hand. He wanted something young and fresh. He wanted a girl but not just any girl. Perhaps a perky little cheerleader. They seemed to be ripe in all the right places. It so happened that the princess was friends with one right there in my class. Convenient and would work well in my game with the princess. If someone was to succumb to my death wiles, I preferred they had a dual purpose.

I walked behind Melany browsing the merchandise. Her cheer skirt was too short by the school standards that I had become familiar with. She was practically spilling out of her shirt as well. She was looking for attention obviously and she had gained mine. After she sat down, and I passed out that mornings test I made my way around the room stalking my prey. Melany had not noticed me as I moved behind her. I looked over her shoulder and found the prefect ploy to get her within my grasps. I smiled, pointing to an answer she clearly had marked wrong on her test.

"I would rethink this answer if I were you. Perhaps something like this," I whispered, closely in her ear before adding," I think that would be better."

My fingers lingered a moment longer than appropriate on her shoulder as I made it evident, I was enjoying her finer features. Pink blushed her cheeks as she spied me before returning her gaze back to her test. Yes, there was interest. I contemplated how to use that interest while the witless students finished their work. After class, Melany approached me as I knew she would. My vessel was handsome from what I had been told on multiple occasion, usually by my unsuspecting victims before they became a meal. She would be no different.

"I don't know what to say," Melany floundered.

"Thanks, would be a fine starter."

Melany dug her foot at the ground trying to find more to say to me. "Thanks. This really isn't my subject."

Ah! Academically, I was obligated to teach the poor girl a lesson. She needed help in English, whereas I would be giving her a new kind of Biology lessons and perhaps more importantly one in human nature. The idea had merit. Tutor the student in the ways of the flesh. I had done so with Barbara successfully. For Melany, I wanted to taste her in a much different, darker way though.

"Perhaps with a little extra help, you would be able to appreciate English more," I offered.

"Maybe," she said, batting her eyes as if to flirt with me.

Baited and ready to be devoured. All I need do was reel her in all the way. So easy that it was not even a sport. Still, dual purpose. I had more than one set of eyes on me. The only one that mattered needed to see the show we were putting on though. Audience of one prickly little princess achieved.

"Perhaps tonight, after classes," I extended the offer.

"That sounds great. I don't know how to thank you."

I smiled pleasantly as I leaned in and whispered, "Well, I am sure we can think of something."

The princess spotted the intrigue I was having with her perky little friend. She gave me such a scornful look that I almost felt the need to pleasure myself right there. Her temper over my plotting was fulfilling. The princess was gripping her desk as if for dear life. I knew had she not been gripping the desk she would have lashed out at me. She knew as well as I did the consequences of that.

The bell rang out and the students began to gather up their books and papers.

"Leave you tests on the desks and I will see you all tomorrow. Until then, read up on the first eighteen pages of chapter nine for an in-class discussion."

The students all groaned and I chuckled. They knew nothing of real hardship. I played my part well though. "I know. I know. Get on out of here."

Melany had waited until she was almost the last one left to walk by me. She smiled coyly, sashaying her bottom as she moved. I gave her a slight wave and a wink as she left. That, of course, was all for show. I had a captive audience of my doomed little princess.

"Why Miss Ruth! Did you have something you needed to speak to me about? Perhaps you are in need of some extra tutoring like your friend," I offered.

Nadine stood tall and firm as she ordered, "I want you to leave me and my friends alone."

"Is that all?"

"I rather you get out of my world all together and crawl back into the dark hole you're from, but it seems there is nothing I can do about that right now," she admitted.

I wanted to infuriate her even more. I wanted her anger but more importantly, I wanted her pain. I couldn't lash out at her directly. That was against the rules. I could mess with her life though. I could lash out at those around her. I just had to keep my follies discreet. I was tired of being discreet though. I wanted to give them all a statement. I wanted to escalate the game already. It was time after all.

"Well, lucky me then. Miss Ruth, I am sorry if you think I have foul intention here at this school. All I want to do is teach this class until Mrs. Brookstone returns. Nothing more, nothing less."

She scoffed and said, "Why do I find that hard to believe?"

"I don't know but until you can prove otherwise, I suggest you treat me with the same respect you treat all your other teachers here or I will be forced to have you removed from my class permanently. Am I making myself clear," I told her with a less than polite smile.

Nadine gritted her teeth seething as she said, "Crystal."

"Good. Now get to class. I wouldn't want you to get a detention on my account, now would I," I told her, shooing her away.

I turned away from her, picking up the papers my students left behind. I could feel the heat of her anger pouring off her. It was such a yummy thing. She didn't say another word as she exited, no doubt to send warnings to her little friend. I was sure she would warn the girl off but lucky for me the teenagers of the Real didn't do much for their own good. I had no doubt my little pretty prey would be at my classroom door at the prescribed time as planned. Mores the pity for her.

Nadine

I was seething mad when I left the classroom. Lou planned on messing with my life. That was abundantly clear. I needed to warn Melany off him but wasn't sure what to say. I couldn't let her be alone with the beast. There was no end to the depths of his scheming. Whatever he had planned for her was not anything good. I knew that for sure. I found Melany by her locker. Still raging from my encounter with Lou, I grabbed her arm pretty roughly, too roughly.

"Hey! That hurts," Melany cried, pulling her arm away.

"What's going on between you and Mr. Jacobs," I demanded.

"Huh, what are you talking about?"

"You heard me. What's going on between you and Mr. Jacobs," I demanded again.

"Nothing. Why?" She was feigning innocence and I didn't have the time or temperament to deal with games.

"Don't nothing me, Melany. I saw him leering at you in class," I barked.

"He was leering. Really?"

It made me sick thinking she actually got off on him leering at her. I knew Melany liked them older, but Mr. Jacobs was a teacher. More importantly, the thing inside Mr. Jacobs was far older and a lot more dangerous. I couldn't tell her any of that though. I had to try to scare her off another way. I still had no idea how or what to say. My anger was all that was coming off.

"Melany, That's not a good thing."

"Says you. I think it's hot that he was taking a personal interest in me. I would do anything to get him alone for just ten minutes," she admitted.

My jaw dropped open. I recovered quickly though and cried, "He's a teacher for Christ sake!"

"I know. He is also the most drop-dead gorgeous thing this school has to offer."

I tried to tell her how crazy he was. I tried to tell her the things Danny and I had learned from researching Mr. Jacobs. As it turned out, Mr. Jacobs was no saint either. He had been suspended before his coma for suspicion of an inappropriate relationship with one of his students. The student actually died in the same car crash that had put him in his coma. It was hinted that they were running away with together. No one knew for sure if that had been true, so the case was dismissed. Melany didn't want to hear any of that though. She was too smitten by the foul beast.

"And you might very well end up that way if you let him get you alone. The man is a psycho," I warned her.

"What? You're crazy," she balked.

"I'm serious. Before he was in the hospital, he -" I tried to convey how serious I was. I had to tell her the whole story.

"Wait! I don't want to hear it, Naddy. I know what this is really all about. You think he is a stud and want him all for yourself. No. Don't. I have seen how you look at him when we are in class. You watch every move he makes. You can't take your eyes off him. Well, let me tell you something. Not everyone's life revolves around you. Okay? You have Carter and you have Josh. Both are smoking hot. Leave Mr. Jacobs for the rest of us. Okay? I am going to get me some of that. You hear? I can see and do whatever I want without your highness getting in my way. So, back off!"

Melany pushed passed me as I was choked for words. Mr. Jacobs came behind me after a moment and I could feel his triumphant smile without even looking at him. A crowd that had formed to watch our drama unfold began to disperse.

"Well, she did get the highness part right at least," Mr. Jacobs whispered in my ear.

I spun around on my heels and said very firmly, "Stay away from me, stay away from my friends. I won't warn you again."

"Oh, that I wish I could, dear princess. I would be a silly fool to pass an opportunity up such as this though. After all, I am a teacher and there are so many here in need of a good lesson or two," he whispered to me before heading down the hall without waiting for a response.

I didn't know what to do. My friend was in grave danger and she wasn't listening to reason. I wished I could tell her the truth. I wished I could tell all of the them truth. I could keep the safe if I was allowed to let them know why they were in danger. I couldn't tell them though. Their lives were all in danger and I couldn't tell them the one thing that could keep them alive. Things were definitely going to get bad before they got worse.

Soubackalou

After school, Melany stood in the classroom with her books against her chest. She brushed at her skirt and fiddles with her hair. All the while, I was watching her as I stood by the door. I smiled folding my arms across my chest. It was going to be so much fun.

"Now here is a surprise," I called out, startling her.

"Oh hi," she said with a tiny gasp.

"Hello, Melany. I didn't expect you to be here."

For a moment she looked confused and a bit disappointed. My indifference was part of the game after all. "Oh, but you invited me, didn't you? I thought you did."

Oh! The mind games I could play with such a wisp of a thing. It would take weeks to break her mind thoroughly, much longer than the ever-buoyant Mrs. Brookstone. Our time was limited though. The princess knew I had sights on the girl. I would have to make quick work of her. Still, that didn't mean I couldn't have some fun while I did so.

"Well, I guess it doesn't matter now. You are here after all and I bet you are eager to get down to business," I said, waving off the presumed miscommunication.

"I want to learn anything you are willing to teach me. I can be an excellent student when I put my mind to it," she said coyly.

Oh yes. It was going to be so much fun. So eager was she, just like my last plaything. She would regret that soon enough.

"I have little doubt in that. Come with me," I told her, reaching my hand out to her.

She took it without regard but asked, "Where are we going?"

Her palm was sweaty and warm in my own. She was nervous and for all the wrong reasons. I had designed a night of red wonders. The stage just needed to be set. She would make for a fine piece of art when I was done with her.

"I find the confinement of the classroom a bit suffocating. I think we can stand for a change in scenery, don't you?"

"Sure. I'm game," she said confidently.

To that, I replied with a chuckle, "No, my dear. You are bait but let's not get ahead of ourselves. Shall we?"

I took her down the hall to the gym. I found that area had the most potential to do the most damage. There were no extracurricular activities that evening so it made for all the more time to play with my new toy. Melany laid her books on the bleachers before wiping the sweat from her palms. I walked past her to the wall where the mats where resting against. I pulled off one of the matts letting it down just enough that we could sit on them. I then turned to my prize and removed my tie.

"I think this is a more relaxing spot, don't you," I asked, with a wink.

"Y-Yes. It's great," she stuttered. Poor thing was nervous. She had every right to be, but I was sure again it was all for the wrong reasons.

I lounged on the mat crossing my legs and beckoned to her to join me. "Come sit down. Don't worry I won't bite. Well, not much at first anyway."

Melany nodded, sitting beside me. Her hands folded innocently in her lap. For a cheerleader, she was more nervous than I through possible. Perhaps the rumors of all the promiscuity within their ranks was untrue. It only made the conquest that more satisfying. Melany realized after a moment she didn't have her books. When she moved to get them, I stopped her taking her hand in mine.

"We don't really need them, do we? I mean, after all, you didn't come here for help in your subjects. Not really. You wanted ten minutes alone with the good Mr. Jacobs. Just ten minutes alone, right? You would do anything for ten minutes alone with me. I am sure it wasn't classwork you really wanted tutoring in, or am I wrong?" She began to stutter again when I placed my hands on her knees. I let my thumbs circle them slowly as I said, "It's okay to admit you want me, Melany. I want you too. It's strange really. I didn't know how much I wanted you until I saw you standing there tonight in my classroom. I know it's wrong and I shouldn't be telling you all this, but I can't help it. I want you so much it hurts."

I turned from her feigning pain. I knew I could release a tear if need be to ensnare my prey. The only pain I was in though was from the hunger inside me. It was not for love but something far more sinister. The perky little cheerleader was falling in line quite easily.

Melany gasped, "Oh my god. I feel the same way. I am like so totally in love with you that it hurts."

"God, I know how you feel but we can't! You are a student and I am a teacher. They will fire me or worse if they found out about us," I said as I turned back to her playing my part.

"I'll never tell," she promised. I knew was that true enough. She wouldn't be telling anyone anything when I was done with her. What was left of her though would tell quite a story.

"We would have to be very careful, Melany. No one could ever know how we feel for each other," I said as I played along with her little love story.

Melany nodded and agreed.

"Good girl. I knew I could trust you." I caressed her cheek with my hand. Such soft skin looking to be sliced, no doubt. "I knew you were the one I needed."

I kiss her lightly at first. My hands gripped her sides, discreetly. The kisses became more fevered. She was enjoying every moment of it. I could feel the heat of passion rising from her. My hands started to roam. She seemed to enjoy that. Her head fell back as I kissed her neck. She gasped when I touched her breasts.

"You taste so sweet. You taste like strawberries in springtime. Your lips are like soft rose petals. I need to taste them again and again."

Melany lapped up every word as if she had hungered all her life for it. It seemed a pity to rip apart something so pathetic but alas, games were at play and my vessel was so very hungry. I kissed her fiercely gripping her arms. Melany winced in pain but didn't stop me until I bit her lip. She pushed me back holding me at arm's length.

"Ouch! That hurt," she whined.

"It was just a love bit. I am sorry if I hurt you, my darling. I just can't seem to control myself around you."

The platitudes seemed to ease her distress. I smiled brining her back into my arms. We kissed some more. Melany let me lie her flat on her back. I ran my hand down her thigh, gripping her. I found her apex then and touched her. She was wet to the touch. I knew she liked my vessel, but I had no idea of how excited being with it had made her. She tried in vain to move my hand. I had found her secret and wasn't letting it go. Eventually, she gave in to my kisses and touches. I explored her like I was sure no man had before. She let me open her blouse and feel the silky material against my fingers. The blush reddened her cheek. Yes, I was correct. The girl was a virgin. My vessel became firm just at the thought of our revelation. My mouth found the silk and devoured it. I gripped the silk and pushed it up revealing her naked form. The lump of breast suckled in my mouth I had no choice but to take a taste. My teeth bit down on her. I must have been a little too rough because she was trying again to fend me off.

"Stop! Stop! You're hurting me," she cried.

I smiled at her struggles. She had no idea what pain was, but I was about to show her. I held her hand above her head and made my intentions known. My arousal took by force what only moments ago she was willing to give. She screamed to no avail. Tears ran freely down her face. I licked them up roaring in triumph as I came to completion. Once I was done, I rolled off of her with a happy sigh. She rolled herself into a ball still bawling like a baby. I patted her leg which only made her cringe in response.

"Poor little thing. It looks as if I broke my new toy too soon. Don't worry, love. You got what you wanted. Perhaps next time you should listen to your friend," I said with a sigh.

She struggled to sit up. I could see I had in fact been rough with her from the bruises already forming on her wrists. The blood between her leg mixed with my spent essence. My little love bite had bled, leaving stains of crimson across her breast. She tried to hide the bits of her I already taken. That made me chuckle. She had acted like the wanton trollop and I gave her what she wanted. Regret was a fool's game. The girl had to die. It was long past due. Not just for my game with the princess but because her pathetic existence warranted it.

"Oh well. Love can be the death of us all. And it certainly will be in your case, my dear. There is more of you I need before this night is through," I told her with a chuckle.

That got her attention. Her face quickly turned to me in shock. I anticipated the frightened cherub 's plan to flee and grabbed her ankle mid stride. I pulled her down to the ground and mounted her again. My hands found her slim throat and squeezed. It didn't take long for the life to leave her broken form. I had such things I had wanted to do to her. Such a waste really. I could still utilize her body for my plans though. That in itself made her worth it.

"Now it's time to set the scene. After all, her highness will want you displayed properly, and we always give the princess what she wants. No matter what."

I pulled my knife from my briefcase that had been lying nearby in wait. I wasn't sure how I wanted to display the broken pieces of the little perky cheerleader, but I knew it would be epic. I looked over the body, cursing myself for not being about to take more pleasure out on its form before I sliced her up. The stains of mascara had ruined her face. That would have to be cleansed before my masterpiece was displayed. I tapped my knife against my chin contemplated my options for display. I couldn't wait until the princess saw my artwork. I had much work to do.

Chapter 21

Nadine

I searched all morning for Melany in hopes of finding her alive and well. I was worried because when I had left her, she was dead set on seducing Mr. Jacobs. She had not picked up any of my calls that evening. All her calls were sent straight to voicemail. My messages went from casual to downright scared for her. I knew she was ignoring me on purpose, but I had to warn her again. Melany had no idea the horrible thing that laid just under his skin, the true demon inside. I tried to warn her, but she had not listened. I knew what Mr. Jacobs really was though. I hoped I was in enough time to double down on my warnings. I feared more than anything I had failed my friend.

Kelly Ann, Sam, and I found some of our mutual friends we shared with Melany the next morning. I asked around, trying to sound subtle. As it turned out Melany was supposed to meet Scott, a friend from History, for a study session. She had stood him up though. She wasn't answering any of her calls or texts again all morning either. That did not bode well. I had a sinking feeling inside me that Melany had met with disaster. The disaster had a name I had come to know as Lou. I didn't want to think about what could have really happened to her. I had been under his control unwillingly. I knew what he was capable of.

"I wonder what got into her. She never breaks a promise," Sam commented on Melany's behavior, confused as to what was happening. I knew though. Damn it all but I knew.

There was a crowd growing near the gym as we made our way down the hall. That in itself was not out of the ordinary. The two police officers stopping students from entering was though. They were trying to close the doors asking the students to avery their eyes. Phones were out trying to take shots from around the insistent officers. Panic filled me. I prayed it wasn't what I thought. I prayed I was wrong as I pushed through the crowd trying to make my way closer. I was so absorbed with trying to get through the throng, I didn't even feel when a hand gripped my arm. The sudden jerk sent my instincts on edge and I almost knocked out the person on the other end. Thankfully, it was only Danny.

"Wait. Don't go in there," he warned.

I could see the look on his face. He was trying to save me from what was just beyond the doorway. Others were peering inside. Some backed away quickly crying, others looking ready to vomit. I knew then it was my worst fear. I had failed my friend and Lou made a very public kill.

"It's Melany, isn't it?" Danny wouldn't even look at me and I knew the truth. I hoped against all hope I was wrong, but I knew I wasn't. Tears formed in my eyes. "Is it her? Please tell me it isn't her."

"She was found her in there this morning by the janitor when he came in. The police didn't want the body touched until they could investigate the scene."

I cried out as if I was the one in pain, as if I was the one Lou had hurt. That time it had not been me though. That time it had been a friend of mine. She had not been my best friend, but she was still a friend. Melany had befriended me the very first day of cheer and because I let her in my life, she was dead. Melany died because of me. Anger bubbled up in me as I clenched my fists. I pushed passed Danny and moved toward the gym. I had to see what I had caused. I needed to know the truth. It was my fault and I needed to see what I had reaped.

"Nadine, wait," Danny yelled.

I pushed through the crowed until I was able to see inside the gym. Blood was all over the mat and floor where the body had been dragged.

<u>Last of the Dream Warriors – Jealousy</u>

Melany's body had been hung under the back board of the basketball net. She had been hung by her entrails. Her face had been beaten, nearly unrecognizable. It was Melany though. She had died a very brutal death and I was to blame. I covered my mouth in tears to hold back the vomit ready to escape. Danny came up behind me and turned me away from the gory scene. I hugged him, crying uncontrollably. He took me to the other side of the crowd away from prying ears.

Danny tried to comfort me. "He'll pay, Nadine. I promise you he will pay."

"It's all my fault. She died because of me, Danny," I admitted.

"Don't ever think that. He murdered her not you."

"He did it to get to me." It was all true. He did it to hurt me and he succeeded. He had not even needed to touch me. All he needed to do was use the tools at his disposal. Lou used my friend against me.

Danny hugged me again, having no words that could comfort me. It was my fault no matter what he or anyone else said. Melany died because she trusted the man, I knew was a killer. Yes, I tried to warn her off. I could have tried harder; I should have tried harder. Because I hadn't, a girl was dead. Lord knows how many others might follow. I couldn't protect her; I couldn't protect any of them. I was failing the Real and most of all, I was failing my friends.

I felt Danny look over my shoulder and tense. I knew Carter must have come through the crowd. The two of them still were not getting along as I would have liked. I turned to see Carter giving Danny a hard look. Carter didn't bother to approach us, heading back the way he had just come. Had I already not been feeling distraught over Melany's senseless death I probably would have been hurt by Carter's behavior. My mind was on Melany though. Kelly Ann hurried over to me in tears as well. She had saw the horrific scene as well. We grasped each other mourning our friend in the senseless tragedy. Danny backed away from us letting Kelly Ann comfort me as I was her. He looked off toward the classrooms. Something caught his view because his fists were balled tightly. His jaw was locked and tense. I looked over to where Danny had been looking but saw nothing. I knew Lou had been there though. I could almost feel his dark aura still lingering. I knew he had been gloating over his handiwork. I didn't care what anyone said. His reign of terror had to end, and it had to end now. As soon as we made our way back to the Realm, I would make sure there was no negotiation in that. Lou was done in the Real or else they wouldn't like the things I did to stop him. I would not see another of my friends be under his murderous grasp again.

That evening, I rushed into the Council chambers and should have been surprised they were all already there. I really wasn't though. Danny was there with my sister and cousin. I put my hands on my hips with a loud sigh of disgust. I wanted to yell and scream at them for not taking me seriously sooner, but I knew I had to focus. There was a process and I would follow it until I had no other choice. It was a matter not for my family but the Council. As it was, the Council was already in their seats waiting patiently for me. I was sure Danny already informed them of what had happened and my state of mind. They had been forewarned but I didn't care. The only thing I cared about was a resolution. Lou had to be banished from the Real and that was the only thing I would settle for. Once he was back in the Realm, I would dispatch my own justice. Screw the punishment.

"I should have figured you'd be here already," I grumbled.

"I informed the Council of what crimes Lou has committed," Danny told me.

"Let me guess. They can't do anything. Right," I barked.

I knew I should be addressing the Council directly, but I didn't. They had failed me and my family more than once already. It didn't matter Gloria was a part of them. She was only one of the seven. Even if she did truly sympathize with me, she was in contest with the others. These were not my favorite people by far, but I needed them. I needed their pull with the SLAG Nation.

Devon cleared his throat before saying, "We are to meet with the SLAG Council in order to inform them of what crimes the Dark Lord has committed and try again to come to an agreement on the entire situation."

"Yeah. Like I said, nothing," I murmured.

That I was met with clicks of tongues and whispers from those in audience. I didn't care. I needed action and I needed it now. People were dying and I could not fathom a different response but Lou being removed from the Real. It had to happen, or I was unsure what I would do.

Xavier sighed saying, "This is not an official Council meeting, princess, so we will not hold you accountable for your words."

"We also know that you have lost an ally recently so we will go easy on you," Gone added.

That didn't set well with me. They were talking about Melany and didn't even know her. What right did they even have to speak of her? "She wasn't an ally. She was a friend. She was a human being."

"She was a pawn in the Dark Lord's plan," Devon agreed.

"And how many more pawns will have to die in order for you to see we have to force the SLAG Nation's hand in this? How many of my friends need to be taken from me in my life, my world," I questioned.

Xavier corrected me by saying, "This is your world, princess. The Real has always been a temporary haven for you."

"Until you find a way to keep me here without jumping between worlds as I have been then it is still my world too. We need to fix this, and we need to fix it now."

The group sat back stunned silent by my apparent anger and words. They all knew I was right. There was little else to say.

A group of translucent floating beings appeared on the other side of the chamber. Everyone turned to them. Four paper thing beings with huge heads floated nearby. Their skin translucent so that the matter underneath was visible. They were all wearing matching gray robes. The SLAG Nation had heeded the call and came to us. Now we were getting somewhere. I had not been witness to any of the real negotiations to that point with the SLAGs. I had let Gloria, under Danny's direction deal, with them directly. Neither Gloria nor the rest of the Council had made any headway. Now, it was my turn. I was prepared to state my case.

"Well here is your chance, princess. Why don't you convey the seriousness of the situation to the SLAG Council? Maybe you will have better luck than we have," Old Mathew offered.

A man who is nearly translucent as the SLAGs stepped forward. He had both SLAG features, but his body resembled more like a human man. His arms were not long and gangly nor was his head as big. Vex, Danny's friend. It had to be. It comforted me some that at least someone Danny knew was here to assist with the process. Vex has always been partial to the human as he had once been one. I prayed he was still on our side in the issue.

"Princess Nadine of Detoriola, this is the SLAG Council interpretation, Vex. Vex, this is princess and heir to the kingdom of Detoriola. She has asked to speak on behalf of the Council of these seven kingdoms," Xavier introduced us.

Vex nodded before saying, "It is my pleasure to finally meet you, princess. I hope this conference will help bring a resolve to the imbalance in the force."

"The Force," I said confused.

"The force is the balance between spiritual powers, good and evil," Unicorn informed me by whispering to me in my ear.

The Force between spiritual powers. It was a battle between good and evil. I was trying to defend two worlds against the evil that was Lou. I just had to make them see that the evil Lou was performing was a greater threat than I was to the Real. It was about the safety of the Real, all of it, including my friends and family.

I nodded in understanding. The SLAGs began clicking and moaning. Vex looked to them and then back to me before saying, "You are the one who all this is about I am told."

Talk about being put on the spot. I wanted to shout that it was all about Lou, but I would be wrong. I was involved, if only as part of Lou's greater plan. I needed to gain their trust. I needed to also stay calm or else I would never be rid of Lou. Most of all, I needed to know they would not take me from the Real. I knew my tether had been a point of pain for many of the Council and my own family. I belonged to two worlds. I couldn't give up either at the moment. I had so much unfinished business.

"I guess you can say that. I am here not just to work this out for the benefit of this world but also for the Real."

"It had been our theory that the situation in the Real would work itself out now that Soubackalou of your Shadowland has taken residence in one of the vessels. Because of his greater access to power we even placed a guardian to walk the Real with you," Vex explained their reasoning.

"And I thank you for that but if Lou had not been sent into the Real, I would not need Danny to be there. It isn't just Lou though out there coming after me. It is other vessels as well," I reminded him.

A look spread across Vex's face quickly before it disappeared. The other demons in the Real were not supposed to happen. It was written across his face. Lou out maneuvered these evolved beings. I could have almost laughed if it had not been so ridiculous. Thankfully Lou had not been using the demons in a way to call attention to himself or them. Maker knows what they were truly up to though.

Vex nodded with a solemn face said, "Yes. That has been unfortunate."

I couldn't help myself because his words were making me angry. "Unfortunate? Is that what you call it? I would say it is more along the lines of unfair."

"It was not something we had planned on. Soubackalou has found a way to obtain other vessels and use them for his own purposes. A loophole, if you will, in the accord. There has been nothing we can do to stop the claiming of the vessels," Vex admitted.

"Then recall him," I stated plainly.

The loud clicks and hisses came from the inhuman beings behind him. Vex listened before looking to us again unable to hide the frown on his face. He disagreed with the SLAGs but couldn't voice that opinion. He was there after all as their voice, not their conscious.

"We still have hopes this will work it out all on its own," Vex told us.

"He has killed. You know that, don't you? He has taken the life of someone in the Real. Possibly several individuals that we know about. Does that not matter to you?"

Vex nodded again and said, "Again, it is unfortunate."

That was not the word to describe what Lou was doing in the Real. What he was doing was horrific. It was barbaric. It was cruel and life altering to so many people. There were so many more appropriate words for what the situation was. Unfortunate was definitely not one of them.

"There's that unfortunate word again. He took a life." The words caught in my throat as I tried to keep calm but was failing miserably. I continued though saying, "She was my friend! She died because Lou murdered her. He murdered her then mutilated her body as a message to me. He will stop at nothing until he does the same to me. This isn't about balancing the force of power anymore. This is about pure and simple revenge."

Clicks came from the SLAGs.

Vex looked to them before turning back to me confused as he said, "Revenge? We do not understand."

Gloria was the one to answer the question using all her royal demeanor and power of the Council behind her. "Soubackalou married the princess's mother while she was pregnant with her. It was the queen's right to will her kingdom to the heir of her choice. Detoriola has a history of the heir to the throne being the last-born female of the bloodline. It was the queen's choice to continue the tradition that Princess Nadine would inherit the throne and not that of her new husband. As you can imagine, he took this very hard."

Samurata scoffed at that. I let it go though, because the meeting was about getting Lou out of the Real, not the opinion of one Council member.

Vex appeared taken aback by this new information. He commented, "This is nothing but a family feud. If we had known of this in the beginning, we would have never allowed Soubackalou off world."

"If the right questions are never asked the true answers can never be found," I told him.

"Well spoken, princess. With the death of this innocent girl and the revelations of today's meeting, I think our people need to discuss this amongst ourselves," Vex stated.

Discuss? I was confused. Did I not just make my case? It was not about balance or whatever thing Lou used to get into the Real. It was about his own selfish games. They needed to see that.

"What's there to discuss? Lou lied to you in order to come at me where he knew none of my people could protect me," I argued.

Danny looked at Vex curiously before saying, "This wasn't about balance of power. Surely you see this."

"Vex, can you not help sway their decision," Gloria asked.

"I understand your situation. Truly I do. This is not up to me though. This is a matter for our full council to agree on." I could see the look of concern in Vex's face. The lines creased more after another series of clicks and moans from the others. "We must go now. You will have our decision soon."

Vex moved back to the SLAG Council and stood before them. They all disappeared through a veil of grey smoke.

I turned to the Council not feeling much was accomplished. It was not a new feeling for me. I needed answers of how we did and if they though the SLAGs would do what we asked. "Now what?"

Gloria sighed before saying, "Now we wait."

"And what about my friends in the Real? What about my family there? Do I just sit back, and watch Lou pick them off one by one until the SLAGs make up their mind?"

Samurata stood before saying, "There is nothing more we can do at this moment. You will have to be patient."

"Patient? You're not serious."

Samurata was already making his way from his Council seat. He was done with me and I could tell. I had turned the rest of the Council against his Dark Lord and that was intolerable to him. I received looks of sympathy from the others but a lot of good that did me. They couldn't help. No one could help. We were on our own in the Real.

"I know how difficult that can be for you of all people, princess but that is exactly what you need to do," Devon stated.

I watched the Council disappear from their appointed seats until all that was left was my family. Gloria came to where Danny, Unicorn and I were standing. She sighed, hugging me. I accepted the hug but only for a moment. Fresh tears were in my eyes. Nothing was accomplished and my friends were still in danger. I didn't do what I had set out to. I was frustrated and filled with shame. Most of all, I was angry Lou still had not paid for his crimes.

"If he comes near me or my friends, I will kill him again. Vessel or not. I will make sure he doesn't have a chance to hurt another soul as long as I live," I informed them all.

"You can't protect them all, Nadine," my sister told me.

"Maybe not but I can try. It is more than anyone else is doing," I told them before turning on my heels and hurrying from the room.

Chapter 22

The fury I was fighting off didn't bode well for cheerleading the next day. I had wanted to call out sick, but Lulu had been up my butt all week about getting the routines down. She had become more insistent since Melany's death. Lulu insisted it was what Melany would have wanted. I was a warrior princess from an alternate reality but as far as she was concerned, I was some insignificant worm who couldn't stick her landings properly. I guess in the bigger picture it was not a tragedy. The tragedy was that we were having a benefit for a girl who died because of me. I was ashamed and riddled with guilt. I was also so very angry. Lou should have been dispatched from the Real already. Turned out, the SLAGs were not a hive mind as previously thought but a regular democracy, not really anyway. The death of one insignificant child from the Real wasn't enough for all the SLAGs to change their minds. The debate continued within the collective much to all our chagrin.

I was standing with Danny on the gym floor waiting for our squad to be queued for our big entrance. The student body was still was converging on the gym. Kelly Ann had made her way over to me gushing over my uniform.

"You make tacky look totes," she told me.

I was about to ask where Carter and Sam were but then I spotted them. I hadn't seen Carter in days and there he was on the top bleachers with Sam and they weren't alone. A sexy little red head was laughing beside them, her hand squeezing Carter's arm. If my fury had not been in full swing already because of Lou, it was now.

I was fighting dead eyed freaks and magical half demons trying to keep the world safe, all while taking shit from my boyfriend for not making time for him. Did I argue about how unreasonable he was acting? No. Did his behavior justify the way he had been treating me? No. Was I upset about him being a jerk half the time anymore? A little but I didn't press him. How am I repaid? He brings a date to my cheer event honoring my fallen friend. I wasn't hundred percent sure it was a date. It probably wasn't but she was definitely putting out vibes he was most certainly picking up. It sure felt like more than friendship from where I stood.

The basketball net above us began to rattle from the amount of power coursing through me. Danny took immediate notice. He pulled me aside telling me to breath. He tried to soothe me with his words.

"What is it, Nadine? What's wrong," he asked trying to diffuse the situation.

"What's wrong? What's not wrong is more like it. I have to stand here while Lou gloats at the fact he murdered a friend of mine and has all but got away with it. I can't do anything about it because he is in a borrowed body. Everything around me is turning to shit and I am at my wits end," I told him. I looked about to Carter briefly seeing him laughing again with the sexy stranger. She leaned in that time, giving him a perfect view of what she had to offer. "What the hell is that about?"

I meant to just motion to Carter and the stranger. My powers had another thing planned though. Invisible energy poured from me and sent the bleachers in motion. They collapsed sending students diving for safety. When the dust settled at the top of the bleachers still stood Carter, but his new friend was not just beside him but holding on to him for dear life. I looked to Danny and growled. Lulu and the squad be damned. I needed to get out of there. Despite a few different people calling after me, I left the gym and headed out to the parking lot. I couldn't go back in there no matter what anyone said. I just wanted to go home. I couldn't just go home though. My grandmother would worry if she saw me home early. Damn it! Why was my life so freaking complicated?

When I stopped, I could feel Danny nearby. I took several breaths attempting to calm down before I turned to him.

"What the heck just happened in there," Danny asked confused.

"I don't know," I said shaking my head.

"It looks like you just used your powers in full view of civilians on purpose," Danny said but added after a brief pause, "Did you?"

"I don't know," I repeated with a shrug.

The look on his face said he believed otherwise. He tried to reaffirm his belief, but I wouldn't admit to that. The ramifications of me having my powers in the Real were too much for me to deal with already. I didn't want it to be true. I didn't want the things that had been happening to be true. I didn't want to be an even bigger freak than I already was.

"What else could it have been? A malfunction in the gears? A few idiots playing a game," Danny asked trying to offer.

I gave him that knowing look. We both knew I was fooling myself. My powers had followed me into the Real. Some odd things had been happening and it was beginning to all make sense. I was the girl from the prophecies. I had could travel between worlds and now I had my powers in both. I sat on a nearby bench with my head in my hands groaning. So much for a normal life in the Real.

"You know this could be a good thing. It could help you against Lou if you can control it," Danny said, trying to shine good into the situation as he sat beside me.

"Well, if that is the case then we will come to that bridge when we do. I just can't deal with this right now. There are more important things I need to deal with first," I told him, standing up.

"What could be more important than the fight with the Dark Lord?"

I just looked at him unable to admit the truth. He was smarter than that though. He stood as well looking ready to give me yet another lecture. It would not be one as educational as so many before though.

<u>Last of the Dream Warriors – Jealousy</u>

"This is about Carter. You can't let this boy run your life. There are more important things happening to be wrapped up in some romantic drama," he yelled at me.

"Back off, Danny. Just back off," I yelled, back storming off.

Danny was not letting it go though. "You need to do what is best for your people. This is not helping," he called after me.

As I took off running back down the hall to escape his tirade, the locks on every locker slammed against the lockers. I didn't want to hear his argument anymore. I wanted all of it to be over already. I wanted to go back to be a normal broken teenager who wasn't endowed with superpowers. I wanted to forget the things I had begun to remember. I wanted my dysfunctional life back.

Carter

Nadine had disappeared after practice with Josh. I shouldn't have been surprised but I was. She knew I had come there to see her practice but left with Coma Boy anyway. I hadn't notice at first though because despite her promise Barbara had found herself by my side on the bleachers. She was not being as discreet as I would have liked. It didn't help I practically had to save her from falling when the bleachers malfunctioned. When I looked up again both Josh and Nadine were gone. I saw them briefly having a heated discussion in front of the school when I went to look for her. By that point, I had had enough and headed over to the pool hall. I needed a drink and Mitch was happy to provide. School was out so why not, right?

Barbara came sauntering in the pool hall shortly after. When she found me, I was drinking myself to oblivion. I was feeling particularly sorry for myself. One of our good friends had been murdered. Nadine had found comfort with Coma Boy and not me. He had been there for her and I had not been. It was a cross of jealousy and guilt that drove me away from her. It drove me from Nadine and right back into the arms of Barbara several more times. I knew I should end it but being so wanted had become an addiction. Barbara had become my dealer and she knew exactly what to say and do to keep me coming back.

Barbara made her way slowly to me. She placed gentle hands on my chest as she said, "Hey, baby. You don't look so good. Are you not feeling okay?"

"Can't put one over on you, can I? What are you doing here," I asked, being a bit more sarcastic than needed.

"I thought you could use a shoulder, you know, to lean on," Barbara said, sitting in front of me.

"How did you know I would be here? Did you follow me," I asked again.

She shrugged, trying to look innocent. She was anything but. I had learnt that firsthand. She said, "I want to take care of you, Carter. Someone should."

We had the same conversation a few times since our deceit had begun. She didn't think Nadine was right for me. She thought I was playing second fiddle to Coma Boy. I was being played for a fool. I knew deep inside me that couldn't be true. Still, the evidence had been mounting pretty high to just that. I shrugged off the idea. No. Nadine would never be unfaithful to me. I was the bastard who couldn't keep it in my pants.

"Listen. I want to be straight forward with you. You are a great guy, Carter. Nadine must be an idiot not to realize how great you are. She has been taking you for granted for a long time now. I don't know if it was this Josh guy or if it was someone else, but she is not the kindly little virgin she is claiming to be. Take it from one who knows. I like you, Carter. I like you a lot. I want to be in your life. If it means being your friend, then I can live with that. I think we can do much better than that though. I think we can provide each other benefits that friends normally don't," she said, running her hands up and down my inner thighs.

I put down my beer and stated firmly, "I am with Nadine."

"And I am not asking you to choose between us. Think of this as a way to let off some of that tension she has got you all wrapped up with. We both get what we want. You get to have your cake and eat it too and I get you, if only for some randy fun. And it could be real fun too. I promise I would make it ever so worth your while," she told me, hugging her body close to mine.

I grabbed her wrists when her hand threatened to touch my crotch, "I can't betray Nadine."

"Why not? It's not like you haven't already, multiple times. Anyway, she has betrayed you," Barbara whispered taking a swipe of my ear with her tongue.

"You're wrong," I moaned, trying to fight her seductive power.

Barbara chuckled, "Am I? This is not a hard decision, Carter. You take it, take me, or leave it. Either way she will still be out there doing God knows what and it doesn't seem like she wants it to be with you. Besides, I already told you, I can keep a secret."

Barbara walked out swaying her tight behind as she goes. I picked up my beer and drained it quickly. I wipe my mouth, trying to decide. Do I betray the only woman I ever loved yet again, or do I go home and take care of my own needs? While Nadine was out there somewhere most likely with Josh. While I played second fiddle to someone who has somehow gained all her attention. I lowered my head avoiding eye contact with Mitch as I follow after Barbara. I knew I would regret it in the morning again but tonight I needed someone to want me.

Chapter 23

Nadine

Carter was not returning my calls and honestly, I couldn't blame him. I had not been the best girlfriend to him since Lou had entered the Real. I looked all over for him to try and make up for it. I checked his house and then the lot just to be sure, but he was not in his usually haunts. I gave up after a couple hours and decided to seek him out once we got to school the next day. Danny found me first though.

I had avoided Danny in the Realm because I knew he would want to discuss the appearance of my powers. I knew he would not say anything to the others until we talked it out first. Still, I knew the man he was would not keep my secret too long from his wife. When that happened, I was not sure what the reaction would be. Most likely not good if I knew my family. Having powers in the Real meant my powers were growing. I was already more powerful than anyone they had ever seen. It made things even more out of balance for them. It was definitely a conversation I did not want to have.

"I didn't see you last night," Danny said, walking up to me.

"I needed some time to think," I admitted, which was the truth.

"I understand. Its not everyday you almost take out half the junior class," he said with a smile.

I smiled too. Danny always knew how to make me feel better. I reached out and brought him into a comforting hug. No matter what craziness was happening around us, I knew Danny had my back. He wanted the best for me and that was enough. We could argue but he would always be there for me. He was a true friend. I mean, what person do you know that would travel into another world filled with peril and hazards to stand by your side? That was Danny.

Suddenly, I felt a tight grip around my arm jerking me away from Danny. When I looked, I found Carter holding my arm roughly. He looked like he hadn't slept for days. He also looked mad. No, he looked pissed and all that was directed toward me and Danny.

"Hey! That hurts," I said, pulling my arm away from him.

"We need to talk. We need to talk NOW," he yelled.

"Fine but you don't have to man handle me."

I had been abused enough in my life. I was not letting Carter get away with what I had to endure with Bart or any of my mother's other boyfriends. Carter may have had a reason to be mad at me but so did I. I had many reasons to be mad.

"Are you alright, Nadine," Danny asked, looking concerned.

"Back off my girl, Coma Boy," Carter warned giving Danny a curt shove.

"Carter! Just stop it," I ordered.

Carter was not having any of it though. He had reached his last straw. He was convinced that Josh was the problem, and he was there lashing out because of it. A crowd was beginning to gather. I needed to diffuse the situation and I had to do it now. I needed to get the situation out of the public eye.

"No. He has been up your butt from day one. He needs to know I am your boyfriend, not him," Carter growled.

"Some kind of a boyfriend you are. You can't even protect her from your own stupidity," Danny scoffed.

Not the thing to say to a raging Carter unfortunately. Carter moved to strike out at Danny, but I stood between them. I placed gentle hands against Carter's chest blocking his view of Danny. Carter was a madman, but Danny was acting no better. They threatened each other from either side of me. I was the only obstacle keeping them from killing each other. I needed to negotiate the situation with the more reasonable side first if I planned to diffuse it. I turned to Danny with a sigh.

"Josh, let me talk to him. Okay," I begged.

"She wants to be with me, Coma Boy, so bugger off," Carter sneered.

Danny shook his head saying, "Not until I know she's okay."

I told Danny I was fine trying to beg him with my eyes since my words were not getting through to either of them. He conceded to my wishes. I silently prayed thanks to him. Danny was always the one with the cooler head. The situation with Carter was no exception. Carter, on the other hand, wasn't quite done picking a fight.

"What? Do you think I would hurt my own girlfriend? Is that it," he pressed.

"You grabbed her awful hard," Danny told him.

"It's none of your business how I grab her. Do you hear me? She is mine," Carter announced loudly.

"Enough! Josh, I am fine. Honestly, I am. Carter and I need to talk. I will see you after school."

Danny bade me goodbye before he slowly began to walk away. I turned to Carter, who was not looking at me. Instead, he was staring after Danny with violence in his eyes. He wasn't hearing me speak to him, questioning his actions. Instead, he was focused on his target. Danny hadn't made it more than a couple steps before Carter let out a primal growl. He pounced on Danny, fists at the ready. The crowd that had gathered to witness our little drama all jumped out of the way.

When I tried to stop the fight, I found myself being held back. I looked to see who had grabbed me, I found myself in the firm grip of Mr. Jacobs, Lou's vessel. I cringed at his evil touch.

"Jealousy is the finest of deadly sins I have ever witnessed in action. Don't you think," he whispered in my ear with an evil chuckle.

"You bastard. What did you do," I cried, struggling against his grip.

"Not much. I just enticed your boyfriend's jealousy of your relationship with Mr. Groves. Seeds of doubt are in full bloom and the scent is so wonderfully delicious," he bragged, breathing in the air around us deeply.

I pulled away finally moving to the brawlers. I pulled Carter from Danny. I held myself between them again. Fire was in both their eyes from the fight. It was not happening. I was not about to let Lou destroy the people I loved in full view of the entire school.

"Enough. I have had it with this petty jealousy between the both of you. There is nothing going on between me and Josh, Carter. Josh, you need to stop thinking I need protection from the people in this world. Now either you two stop this right now or I will be damned before I talk to either of you again," I yelled.

"Do what you want. I don't even care anymore," Carter growled before stomping off.

I turned to Danny who could only shake his head. I couldn't fault him. He was only defending himself. He was only defending me. Carter was out of control and it was my fault. I let Lou get to him. I let the seeds of doubt about how I felt for him take hold. I had to make things right but had no idea how.

As the crowd was dispersing, we heard the shrill happy voice I had come to dread. "One moment you two. Fighting in school is not acceptable. I think detention is in order. Miss Ruth, Mister Groves, report this afternoon to detention with me in room three."

"That's not fair! I was the victim and Nadine didn't do a thing," Danny argued.

"I think it is fair enough unless you want suspension. That would leave Miss Ruth all alone and vulnerable. We wouldn't want that, now would we," Lou gloated.

I sighed, knowing we could only agree to the detention. Lou had us cornered and he knew it. Lou walked away smiling.

"Do you have the feeling like we are being set up," Danny asked.

"I have no doubt in my mind that we are being set up," I told him, knowing without a shadow of a doubt I was right.

"What do we do now?"

"Play Lou's game and beat him at it," I told him.

We knew it was a trap. It did not matter though. Carter's life was on the line. If Josh and I didn't show up for detention with Mr. Jacobs, he had made it clear. Carter would pay for my indiscretions. It may be a trap, but we had an ace up our sleeve Lou was unaware of. He had no idea my powers were a reality in the Real. We could handle anything Lou threw at us. I was sure.

I arrived at the classroom for detention and entered cautiously. Lou was leaning on the desk with that ever-present evil grin. There was no other soul to be found. He raised his arms gleefully as he said, "Welcome to detention, Miss Ruth. Why don't you have a seat and we can talk about what brought you here today?"

"Oh, I think we both know what brought me here today. Why don't you drop the pretense, Lou? It's just us travelers here after all," I told him.

"You are right. We will drop the pretense, but I think I had asked you to sit down. Now I am telling you. Sit down, princess," he said.

I felt it in my belly before the rest of me did. I was being pushed back by power, Lou's power. I tried to grab a nearby desk but couldn't get any purchase. I ended up skidding my way against the wall. He had his palm pointed at me sending waves at me to keep me where he wanted me. It looked like I was not the only one who had access to their powers in the Real.

Danny came rushing in the room when he heard the commotion. I screamed for him but one moment he was there, the next not. Lou had his hand raised where Josh had been.

"We were having a private discussion, plebe. Mind your betters," Mr. Jacob said in the direction Josh had flown.

"Enough," I cried.

I pushed back against his power with such force he was lifted off the ground and hurdled into the blackboard. The board splintered from the force, bits falling on top of his unconscious form. I hurried to Danny, who was sitting up against the lockers shaking his head. By the time I helped him up, we realized we were not alone.

There were three in front of us and two behind. The dead eyed vessels of Lou's minions had surrounded us. They had boxed us in without us even realizing it. Each creature held a long pole. I sighed, looking at them.

"Five armed halfwits against two unarmed travelers. Do you really think those odds are even," I asked. I held out my hands and willed the poles to me. They came flying out of the minion's hands into my own. I quickly tossed one back to Danny, who in turn readied himself for battle. "Now they are."

We took the minions to school, laying them out one by one with our poles. Once we were sure they were all incapacitated, we dropped out poles breathing deeply. Danny looked to me as I to him. We both nodded before hurrying off into the near empty parking lot.

All of me wanted to go back in there and vanquish Lou again. Danny had been right though. We had no idea what would happen to the vessel if I did that. There were proper ways these things were handled. I couldn't let myself become judge and jury, though after everything I had been through not many would blame me. Still, Mr. Jacobs had done nothing to enlist my wrath. We had to be better at the game Lou was playing. If not, others would start getting hurt or worse, killed like Melany.

Chapter 24

There was a commotion when I arrived back at the palace. Gloria was addressing my sister and her advisors in what looked like a hurried fashion, which was totally not like her. She rarely was anything but proper at all times. That had me curious. I would not have to wait long though to find out what was going on though.

Danny spotted my entrance and rushed to me up. I was still having a hard time with my landings. I could tell he was excited.

"What is going on, Danny," I asked as he wrapped his arm through my own.

"The SLAGs have made a decision. They will be here within the hour," Danny explained, trying to contain his excitement.

I was not sure if they were all excited because of the decision or the fact the SLAGs were on their way. It would not be their first visit to our kingdom or to address the Council. It was a rarity though, which I supposed was the real reason why everyone was in such a state.

"Did Vex give you any idea what the verdict is," I asked in whispered tones to Danny.

If Vex would reveal anything about the SLAGs intentions, it would be to Danny. They had a unique friendship between the two born out of a thirst for knowledge. The bond meant Vex could hold Danny in confidence.

"No. I have not spoken with him. This visit came from the SLAG Council directly. I am not sure he even knows the decision yet."

The SLAGs did nothing that was not planned and thought out thoroughly before hand. If Vex was in the dark on the decision, there was a reason for it. It made me very apprehensive about their visit. Lou had already taken at least one life we knew about and with Mr. Anderson still missing, I had a feeling there were more bodies out there we were most likely going to stumble upon sooner or later. There was logic behind his eviction. The SLAGs saw things at a larger scale though beyond anything we could comprehend. They didn't work with emotion or petty jealousy. Logic and balance were their only tools. They had found logic in sending Lou into the Real. Would they see how off balance he had made the Real because of it?

It made me also think of what Danny had said. If they eviction Lou from the Real, it was possible they may do the same to me as well. I wasn't ready for that. I couldn't leave without saying goodbye to my friends and family there. I couldn't leave the Real with Carter and I on such bad terms. More importantly, I didn't want to leave. I wasn't ready to give up the Real. I wasn't sure if I ever would be ready though.

"Cousin, please join us. There is much to discuss before our guests arrive," Gloria called from the throne.

Danny pulled me along to stand beside Gloria as she continued to address the servants for the impromptu visitors in route. I watched in awe. One day, the title was supposed to be mine. I would have a whole kingdom to command. I would have to know what to do in situations like that and be there to direct everyone on how to handle them. It was an impossible feat, but Gloria dealt with it every day without complaint. I would never be as good at it all as she was.

Eventually, Gloria turned to us with a muted smile. She was exhausted and our visitors had not even arrived yet. "I will have to address the SLAGs as a member of the Council. That means you will be responsible for showing them every hospitality afford a guest of the kingdom in my stead."

"Me," I shrieked certain she could not be serious.

"You are the heir to the throne, Nadine. As a Princess of Detoriola, it falls to you to be the example the people will follow," She confirmed.

I looked down at myself and the very first thing that came to mind was I needed an outfit change. I was wearing a fit pair of jeans dusty from travel and a worn shirt. It was not proper princess attire in the least bit. I may not be able to change my inner deficiencies, but I could fix my outer ones fairly easy enough.

 Dressed in a deep purple gown and wearing my royal bobbles, I stood by the empty throne awaiting our guests with my hands crossed in front of me. Just a step below me was Unicorn and Diana. Diana was wearing a gown as well but hers was forest green. Unicorn, on the other hand, was in full military gear to show her place in the assembly. Down another step was Antonio and Danny. Both men were dressed in formal attire. Gloria was already gathered with the Council in their chambers awaiting the arrival. I was curious why AJ was not present. Technically, he had no official purpose, but he was family by marriage. There was a time and a place for dealing with AJ. The SLAGs meeting was not it. I had to push thoughts of AJ out of my mind. We had a contingency of SLAGs heading our way and I had to mentally prepare.

A slight commotion sounded outside the throne room before the doors were pushed open. Vex stepped into the room first, his head bowed down showing his position as servant to the SLAGs. Behind him three SLAGs came gliding in. Their translucent skin almost glowing in from the lighting in the room. When they were close enough, I rattled off my official greetings to them with apologizes that my cousin was not there to greet them personally. There were click and screeches from the SLAGs.

"Thank you for having us, Princess. We only wish that our meeting was under different circumstances," Vex relayed.

"As do we all. It is our hope though you come baring good tidings," I said hoping for the best.

"Perhaps. We would meet your Council now and ask since these affects you so dearly that you are in attendance," Vex offered.

I nodded, directing them to the Council chambers. The SLAGs began to click and screech again before making their way to the chamber. Vex waited for their retreat before adding, "Daniel of Haasfolk should also join us as he is a traveler as well."

He turned and followed after his masters.

Danny and I looked at each other than to the others. I was happy Danny would be there with me. If nothing else, I would have a friend by my side no matter what they said. I would hope for the best though. I had to. Lou could not remain in the Real, no matter what the costs. If that meant I would also finally be evicted from the Real, then so be it. I couldn't not let any more people die because of me.

Danny and I walked in together spying the Council, behind their marble perch, greeting the SLAGs formally. Vex stood before them translating. I was so nervous I hadn't even realized I grabbed Danny's hand for support. Gloria gave us a funny look but immediately turned her attention back to the SLAGs.

"Dear Council of the seven kingdoms, we present ourselves before you today to provide you with the decision of the SLAG Nation in regard to Lord Soubackalou of the Shadowland. After much deliberation the SLAG Council has found that Lord Soubackalou's entry to the Real is to be revoked based upon the crimes committed on the citizens of the Real," Vex stated for all to hear.

I took a sigh of relief. They were revoking Lou's privileges in the Real. It was what we had wanted since the beginning of that nightmare. He would no longer have access to hurt the people I loved in the Real. He had lost this battle. I looked to Danny who looked concerned instead of happy. When Vex began to speak again I found out why.

"As Lord Soubackalou found a loophole in our arrangement to admit his minions into the Real and has been allusive in locating, we leave it up to your Council to apprehend the lord and hand him over to the SLAG Nation for proper punishment. Once he has been apprehended, we can remove his ability to travel and with that his minions," Vex continued.

Apprehend Lou? How exactly could we do that? What did all that mean? I listened to a debate on just that between the two Councils. As it seemed, I would be granted a boon from them to remove a traveler from the Real, but the boon was limited to only twice. That I could handle. None of them knew I was empowered in the Real so what they thought would be a hardship would actually be much easier with that boon.

"Once Lord Soubackalou has been handed over and the minions are proven to be revoked, Daniel of Haasfolk must also return to a normal life and no longer be a traveler as well," Vex stated.

It was not surprise but I felt a sadness build inside me. yes, Danny being in the Real had been difficult, especially on my relationship with Carter, but it had also been a blessing to have someone with me who knew what I was going through. I would miss being able to unload all my hardships to him in the Real. I had to remind myself I still had Danny by my side though. He would always be there for me in the Realm.

"What of the Princess of Detoriola? Will she be allowed to blatantly do as she pleases in the Real as well," came a voice I recognized all too well. Samurata, with his blood red skin and black eyes. God, but I hated that halfling.

Clicks and screeches came from the SLAGs. Vex looked perplexed for a moment before he turned to address the Kingdom Council again.

"The SLAG Nation can only intervene when laws of man have been broken. The princess and her ability to travel was not a gift given by man but by the Crystal. Her traveling is beyond what we are capable of intervening on. So long as it is her choice to do so, the Princess will do so by the divine authority given by the Crystal," Vex informed the Council.

That set the room in commotion. I stood there stunned. It was not that they would not stop me from travelling to the Real, they couldn't. They were incapable of taking me out of the Real. My odd connection to the Crystal, the ability to travel, my unique powers. It was all from the Crystal, like it was a living thing. Perhaps it was. Who knew for sure? All of that did not matter though. I didn't have to leave the Real. I was safe and soon so would the Real.

I hugged Danny, suddenly overwhelmed with emotions. He chuckled, hugging me back. When I finally looked up amidst the arguing Council members, I saw Gloria staring at us again. Her face looked taken aback but only for a moment. Again, she remembered her royal duties and re-engaged in the arguments occurring about what the SLAGs just told us. Eventually though, the SLAGs had enough of kingdom politics.

"Enough. Our last piece of business is to endow the Princess with the ability to recall a traveler. Please, if you will, Princess. Present yourself to be endowed," Vex motioned for me to come forward.

I stepped closer to Vex cautiously. He smiled lightly, his overly large eyes making cringe inwardly. He placed a long boney hand on my shoulder before turning me to the SLAGs. He leaned toward me whispering in my ear, "The SLAG Council needs you to accept the gift they are endowing to you. It should not hurt from what they have said."

I acknowledge the gift and waited. The lead SLAG glided forward. The stick like arm raised above my head. Its five fingers palmed my skull in its entirety. I closed my eyes and waited. I felt a warm sensation from the touch. After a moment, the hand moved away, and I heard clicks and screeches from the SLAGs. They sounded angry or perhaps confused.

I looked to Vex puzzled and asked, "Did it work?"

Vex listened for a moment also looking confused before saying, "It seems the power was already inside you. Another gift from the Crystal it would seem."

I stood there, stunned. I had the power all along to eject Lou from the Real and had not known it. All the carnage could have been avoided had I knew what was gifted to me from the Crystal. Had my family not been afraid of what I might remember or what I had the possibility of becoming I might have been able to spare the life of my friend. I could not look back and wonder what if though. I had the power to stop Lou. All I had to do was find him, get him along and send his sorry ass back to the Realm, right into the hands of the SLAGs. First, I had to find him though.

Chapter 25

Lou had been allusive all day. It was as if he knew his time in the Real was numbered. I had been performing with my cheer squad when it happened. I felt him before I saw him. From the top of the pyramid, I saw Lou talking by the doors with Kelly Ann. When they both left the gym together, I had no choice. I flipped to the beat of the song with the other cheerleading girls. It was the first time I had been able to land the move perfectly but there was no time to celebrate. I had to stop Lou from hurting Kelly Ann. I began moving toward the doors with that intent. Lulu grabbed her arm stopping me in my pursuit though.

"Where do you think you are going," Lulu demanded.

"I am not feeling so well," I lied.

"Bull. Get back to your slot," she ordered.

"Listen, Lulu. I am sorry but I have to go." I didn't have the time to waste. Kelly Ann's life was on the line.

"I don't care if you are sorry or not. If you leave you are off the squad."

I sighed before saying, "Do what you have to do then."

I walked away from Lulu and found Danny in the crowd. I called out to him and he stood up. Pointing to the door, I call out Mr. Jacobs name. He nodded and moved to the closest door to assist. I kicked the doors open and hurried after Lou and Kelly Ann. I was not surprised to see him standing there holding Kelly Ann by her neck. She was tucked in front of him like a shield.

"Let her go, Mr. Jacobs," I said in a firm voice.

Mr. Jacobs laughed before saying, "Why play these games, Nadine? Why hide all of these secrets from the ones you love? Tell them. Tell Kelly Ann what you really are."

"Leave her out of this," I yelled at him.

Kelly Ann looked scared. I could relate having been at the hands of that particular madman before. She squirmed which only made him more excited.

"What's going on, Nadine," Kelly Ann asked, fear dripping from her voice.

Lou mocked us by saying, "Yes. Tell her what's going on, Nadine. Tell her or I will."

I shook my head, unable to say the words they both wanted me to. I was unable to tell Kelly Ann the truth, even with her life in danger.

Danny came around the corner behind Lou. He skid to a halt, hands drawn up and ready for battle. "Let the girl go. There is no way you can get out of this."

Lou looked to Danny and then back to me. "Does his woman know about you two? I am sure she sure would want to know."

Josh gritted his teeth as he said, "Leave Gloria out of this, you bastard. This is between you and us."

"Fair odds. Don't you think?"

"Why don't you let Kelly Ann go and we can finish this. Don't be such a coward hiding behind a little girl," I taunted him.

Was it a good idea to taunt a maniac? Probably not, but I needed him off guard. I needed him to make a mistake and I didn't know any other way that threaten his manhood. I needed to put him as off balance as we had been for the last couple of months. So, I mocked the powerful dark lord. As it so happens, my plan worked.

Lou knocked Kelly ann on the back of her head and bellowed, "I am no coward. I am a god."

Kelly ann fell to the ground unconscious. As much as I wanted to help my friend it was better, she was unconscious. It gave me the freedom to do what needed to be done unhindered.

"Not in my world you ain't," I told him, raising my hand toward him.

Lou punched the air, sending me hurdling back. From behind him, Danny grabbed him trying to wrestle him to the ground. Lou tossed Danny over, standing over his stunned form triumphantly. I found my opening. I waved my hand out at Danny. He banged into the wall. Standing, I wave my hand again, sending him into the other wall like a rag doll. I let him hoover in front of me just inches from the ground. Danny stood and backed away from Lou.

"By order of the council of the 7 Kingdoms, I hereby order you back to the Realm, never to return the Real," I informed him.

Lou laughed, "You don't have the authority. The SLAGs let me be here."

"Not anymore. The Council has made a new arrangement with the SLAG Nation. You are finished here," Danny told him.

"Thanks for the warning."

Danny scoffed, "She isn't warning you. She is telling you because you are caught."

Lou sneered, "No. What you caught is some poor coma patient whose time is up in this world. I, on the other hand, am out of here."

"Not quite," I said holding out my hand.

The energy flowed through me. I wasn't sure how or why, but I knew that energy was different from my normal powers. It was thicker, stricter than my raw power. I was sending Lou back to the Real for good. Lou's eyes grew big for a moment as the energy encased him before his head sagged. I lowered my arm and the body fell to the ground next to Kelly Ann.

"Bastard!"

Danny came to me, putting a hand on my shoulder in comfort before saying, "Don't worry. It's over now. He is back in our world and can't hurt the people here."

That reminded me. I moved to Kelly Ann. I checked her head and found no blood. At least she had not been hurt too badly. Kelly Ann moaned. It was when I looked at Danny with relief, I saw we were not alone. Sam was standing behind us looking completely freaked out. I nodded to Danny, who turned to see Sam as well.

"What the hell is going on here," Sam asked in shock.

I sighed standing up as I said, "That is a very good question."

Danny got right to the point and asked defensively, "Sam, what are you doing here?"

"I followed you out of the gym when I saw you go after Nadine. Then I saw - I have no idea what I just saw."

I moved to stand in front of Sam blocking his view of the scene. I put a hand on his shoulder, ignoring his cringe. "I know you have a lot of questions, Sam. I will answer them all for you but first we need to get Kelly Ann to the nurse's station."

Danny muttered, "And we need to get our story straight."

Sam asked bewildered, "What story?"

"Just don't tell anyone anything. Okay, Sam? We will handle this. In fact, why don't you meet us by Miss Pauline's office? We will get Kelly Ann help."

I watched Sam go through a full internal debate before he nodded. He was in deep thought, but I knew his main concern was Kelly Ann. Sam headed off to wait for me. When he was out of sight Danny and I dragged Kelly Ann down to the nurse's office. Danny opted to wait outside while I went inside with her. Danny stood outside the nurse's office keeping guard just in case. I walked back out once I knew she was safe and stood beside Danny.

Danny asked after a moment, "What now?"

"Well, I guess we have to decide how much I tell Sam," I replied.

"What do you mean how much? Why tell him anything?"

"We can't just make him go away. He saw something that he can't understand. Sam won't just let it end with me saying, 'I can't tell you.' We have to tell him the truth," I barked.

I knew it was time. I would tell them the truth. It was the only way. I wasn't sure how much any of them really saw but I knew I couldn't keep the lies up anymore. I would start with Sam and go from there. I hoped my friends would accept me after they found out the truth. It was my biggest fear in all of it. I didn't want to lose the people I loved in the Real, but the secrets had driven a wedge between us. It was the only real solution. Despite Danny's protests and regardless of what the Council said, I was going to break my silence and damn the consequences.

BE ON THE LOOK OUT FOR THE NEXT CHAPTER OF THE STORY:

LAST OF THE DREAM WARRIORS

BOOK 4

THE 7 KINGDOM TREASURE